More Mona

Rob J Blevins

Chapter 1

Noel

Noel Kensington stuttered too much, spit when he talked, and said the words, "come again" nearly every time he tried to have a conversation. Yet, he never had any problem giving a lecture in a science classroom. He paced back and forth inside the Chemistry Lab at the University of Nebraska. Each step he took was a solid stomp followed by the pitter patter of his tiny, overly-energetic niece running from one side of the room to the other, tiptoeing lightly over the front domes of his work boots.

It was an extra-credit-day of learning— one that was optional and not sanctioned by the rigid rules the institution. Many students had grades that were slipping, so they leapt at the chance to finish the class with better marks.

Noel wore a bright, pristine white lab coat, and throughout his lecture the lilting sound of his Northern Isle accent mirrored the ebb and flow of the tides. Some British students despised every *Irish-sounding* syllable and perceived mispronunciation of the deep mysteries of the periodic table. But Noel knew science more intimately than the average professor. He drew symbols on the digital work projector that seemed to many like a chasm of unlearned cuneiform. But the room was not full of critics alone. One young lady looked up at him with what seemed like a genuine admiration for his intense regard for science. Either that, or she was American and found his accent endearing.

Noel was filling in for his friend and colleague Ricardo Ramirez for the week while Ricardo took an unscheduled sabbatical in Greece. That lucky lay-about was always getting away with things like unscheduled trips, but helping Ricardo out meant Noel could spend time with his sister's family, who lived in the area.

Halfway through class, Noel stepped out into the hallway to take a breath. Sometimes teaching was like talking to walls. If this bunch cared so much about their education, how come there was never any real interaction in the classroom? If they understood the material, why couldn't they expound on basic topics? He often felt like a clown, performing only the sad pantomime of what an actual professor should be doing, his students merely mute puppets with painted-on faces. He chalked up the impotent feelings and the lack of proper interaction to the fact that he was filling in, and he had determined his students just wanted to get it over with. The feeling was mutual.

"Noel! I sure got lucky you're in the hallway," came a voice.

When Noel looked up, he saw his sister loping in from the parking lot. "Lindsey! I was beginning to think you'd never make it. She's in the classroom. Let me go get her." Noel was glad his sister had interrupted his thinking session that was supposed to be a break. He had just noticed that his whole time in the hallway had been spent flowing from complaint to complaint in his ever-racing mind. "What's that in your hair?" His deep brown eyes crossed as he reached for something tiny clinging to her blonde and greying bangs. "It looks like a twig of..." He sniffed it. "Pine?"

"You have a good nose—that's from the Christmas tree at the Elementary school. The class' pet cat ran three rooms away to the storage room and climbed inside a Christmas tree. I found her shaking there during recess."

"Oh, yes! You have a gift for wrangling tiny, mischievous creatures. I'm going to retrieve *your* little work of art from my science class." He opened the door and the students let out a burst of laughter as the mischievous work of art in question, his very own niece, who was supposed to be quietly coloring in one corner of the room, was now stood atop Noel's desk wearing a notebook over her head. Paper was strewn about the floor, and Noel fumed immediately. "Lucy Renee! Get off that desk! And stop encouraging her, class! Oh, this is impossible!" He began picking the papers up off the floor as she gently climbed down and ran outside to her mother who stood behind the door holding her hand over her mouth.

"Really, Lindsey! This is no time to feel proud. She should know better," Noel grumbled. His sister just chuckled at his lifelong inability to calm down for minutes after something upset him. She couldn't hold back her laughter as she peered downward at Noel bent over retrieving pens and papers from the floor.

"Yes, Noel, she will get a stern talking to." She laughed. "I swear."

Noel reminded himself that he *appreciated* the time he was getting to spend in Nebraska with his sister for the first time in years. His temper simmered. He had met Ricardo years ago when visiting his sister and had kept in touch for close to ten years. Though Noel made his permanent residence in Chicago, Ricardo only taught in the windy city half the calendar year and stayed in this little slice of heaven the rest of the time.

"*Now,* where was I?" The hurricane that

was his niece was over and he stood up quickly letting out a grunt of back pain which made the students laugh even harder. He wanted to cry but he held it in. Old age was no laughing matter. He rattled on ever so quickly hoping that the information went over their heads and they would scramble to take notes or merely miss it all. With each passing day he cared less and less whether this bunch passed or failed. If they wanted to get it over with, well, then, that is precisely what they'd do.

Hours later as the sun was setting, Noel finished up class and jumped into the silver Jetta rental, suavely whisking out his keys and plugging them into the old-fashioned, outdated key start ignition. He turned on the satellite radio to some beautiful raspy young lady singing the same song he had heard a million times. He made a drum of the stirring wheel as he listened to Indie Folk, the short pop of a tambourine accentuating the beat. Someone had inlaid it perfectly into the song as if it was a sugar shaker putting drops of sweet crystalline particles on a tart biscuit. He mused to himself that he didn't understand a word of the song, but none-the-less was hoping he would get reception the whole way to his cabin.

He was staying comfortably in the woods and knew that this was just a steppingstone in his life. He didn't want to be in rural America. Instead, he'd rather be back in the U.K. with all his higher paid classmates. And, he had no frame of reference to know what the woman on the radio looked like, but like most single men he had determined he would spend the rest of his life with her from the sound of her singing voice. He had dated a few women in his time, and the ones that he did were all happily unable to carry a tune in a bucket. It was in this that he equated the inability for most women to carry their life in a civilized manner. He was trying not to be sexist, but he was a well-educated and intelligent man who had been shunned for three solid years by the opposite sex. Ideas of conspiracies of the monarchy flew threw his mind. The blood was boiling in his head nearly every day and it was all he could do to avoid thinking about sex altogether. After all he was a man with purpose.

For the past weeks, he had asked himself what his purpose in life was after all. Was it simply working on teaching students to pay attention? Gathering followers on Facebook? Reaching out to his family? His father was back in Chicago getting tired of giving him things. He had thought that a son who had gotten a doctorate in applied physics and mechanical engineering would be paying to keep a roof over his head. But Noel was always working to be more modest. While his classmates had pursued such advanced careers and worked so much harder, he applied his time to writing advancing theories and developing new approaches to the field. His latest book had won scads of awards in the field, but it gained him no notoriety and people still had no idea of his worth as a scientist. Ideas didn't fix the water heater when it broke and it wasn't as though an academic like Noel had the know-how to fix it himself.

So, secretly, Noel had told himself this trip would be more than time spent with his sister and niece. It would be more than helping out a pal. It would be more than doling out lectures to a class of ungrateful, privileged kids who would eventually forget him. This trip he would learn just what his purpose in life really was.

The sun was about to set as it was six o'clock on the nose. He parked the rental along the gravel road next to his University-provided cabin. He barely planted his leg firmly enough to hold his weight as he wobbled out of the toy car. After doing a European waddle on the gravel, he made his way out of the prehistoric rockpile, and he had determined walking on it all was a barbaric act. Oh, how sweet of them, to think about me and my comfort, he sarcastically quipped to work his mind through his desperation and into his fall chalet. Although nature had painted a striking autumn portrait that was a decadent masterpiece—rich with hues from all over a deciduous palate—all he saw was the inside of his overwrought cerebral storehouse.

He creaked up the porch and heard all the wood cry out as if it wasn't made for humans to walk on, and it was lamenting the very fact. Every piece of the cabin squawked like a bird someone had disturbed or an elderly person that had just had the chair pulled out from under them. He pulled the door open and bells rang. He wondered what the point of hanging bells on the cabin was since he knew he was the only person going in and out. It infuriated him even more to see when he flicked the light switch that the housekeeper had put His and Hers heart towels on the bed. It immediately gave him indigestion and he had barely eaten any food all day. He reached in his pocket and pulled out a tums and made his way to the rocking chair.

The rocking chair wasn't the most comfortable of chairs after standing on your feet all day. He always came home and fought to keep it steady but today he had decided to tap into his resourcefulness. He pulled two huge stacks of hardback books from the provided *library* shelf and mused over their hideous titles. He knew that it was fodder for redneck entertainment. Each pile had three large books and he then stacked them in front of the rocking chair propping his weary feet up on the wasted words that people had decided to publish. Where were the classics? Where was the poetry? Oh yeah, all the poetry he could find was faux transcendentalist romance from the guestbook—men trying to sentimentalize a seventy dollar a night getaway for the mismatched women doing them a solid for life.

He grabbed a half-soaked napkin from the table that had been his coaster and pulled out his pen from his lab coat pocket. He reeled over how he had placed urgency over comfort by not even removing his lab coat to relax. From his acerbic amygdala he conjured up a creative dart board by drawing a stick figure of Ricardo lounging on the beach. What he didn't know was that, meanwhile in Greece, Ricardo looked just like the *Figura* in Noel's picture. He got so many of the details correct by accident—the sagging hammock, the blazing cigar, the pudgy body that was a cheat to his Stick Figure Art Deco. He put a thought bubble above the caricature and expletives that said "%$*& Responsibility!" Noel put the napkin back down and dozed off in the most uncomfortable position of his adult life.

He woke up ten minutes later to the books slipping from his feet and sending his rocking chair into a tizzy. He leapt out of the chair and steadied himself with a corner table which wasn't sturdy enough to hold his body and it shook so much that it spilled a two-day old coffee all over the rug below. The alarm of losing his pay to an unpaid rental deposit woke him up harder and faster than the whole accident put together. He grabbed some wadded-up newspapers from the fireplace and started to soak up the black coffee—a drink already historically attributed to psychopaths.

After throwing some dishwashing detergent and paper towels on the rug—he decided his punishment was to throw his lab coat in the hamper and incarcerate himself on the unmade bed with some cheap, Southern American sub fiction.

At the end of one hour of filling his mind with badly composed fluff, he tried to devise an escape plan from the single life for another solid, dark hour before his thoughts finally wove into nonsense and took him to dreamland at some random beat of the ripe old nine o'clock hour.

Chapter 2

Mona

Mona was twirling with reckless abandon. The lights spread themselves usefully in all directions becoming large polka dots on each person's face and swelling back into the size of a pin hole. The colors were going through their cycle from red to green to blue. Strobe lights were pulsating with the bounce of the compression on the speakers. The sound was maximized for anyone who wanted to challenge their hearing for the rest of their lives. It was a dark and sweaty night club. No one noticed each other's body odor and the smell of a hundred perfumes and colognes blended into a postmodern musk. It was like a wicked flower garden that did nothing to cover up the smell of electronica dancing. Had someone just walked into the club, they would think it was a rave, but that was long decades past on this side of Chicago. The club had a check-in section for the guest's coats and valet cards. Every patron would wear enough to fight the cold chill of fall wind gusts and disrobe into their form fitting dance apparel when they finally made it through the long line outdoors.

Mona's sequin dress was sleek and form fitting. Though her athleticism, raw confidence, and willingness to completely lose herself on the dance floor often attracted others to her side, she was never there for them. She was just dancing to pour out little servings of her soul that night. And if you bothered her, you were met with the ice of a cold shoulder.

She went out alone and carried with her enough Krav Maga training to kill someone, just in case.

"Buy you a drink?"

There was suddenly a masculine voice in her ear, and she flinched, afraid tonight was the night she'd have to test her nose-breaking prowess after all, but as she surveyed the man who was asking, he didn't fit the general description of a creep. In fact, he looked professional—doctor or lawyer type—and honestly, she had a soft spot for doctors. She could let this one down gently.

"No, thanks. I'm about to meet my boyfriend," she shrugged, "but that blonde at the bar hasn't stopped looking at you the whole time you've been here."

He whipped his head around and noticed the barfly blonde who shyly looked away. "Thanks for the tip—I owe you one!"

Like clockwork, the man scattered away

from her. She returned to the groove as before, but the energy drink she'd consumed earlier was beginning to wear off and she took to peeking at the new couple she'd had a hand in pushing together. They looked drunk off something that wasn't wine. It made her roll her eyes. Mona had viewed romance as a disease since she was a little girl. Nothing traumatic had brought her to this conclusion, just her straight-up independence and otherworldly desire for self-control.

Her best friend Monique was calling her phone every five minutes and sending dozens of recorded attempts to get a lifesaver toss from her. Mona Lawson's phone was in do not disturb mode, just like her ambition for the past twenty-six years. She finally slowed her jittery body expressions to a manageable sway which led her to realize she needed to get off the floor before someone mistook her for a teenage couple at a high school dance.

She walked frantically to get outside and just stood in the night air allowing some secondhand smoke to take away seconds of her life. She had over analyzed long ago that it was the guilty pleasure of the non-smoker to do something worse than smoking and just get a whiff through the nose to deal with stress. It reminded her that her willpower was supreme

Czar of her life, and it gave her an invincible feel to know that she could take or leave cigarettes. She was no slave to addiction. Her one avenue for release was coming to this club.

A jaguar pulled up to the curb about five feet from her feet. "Hop in babe!" Out from the tinted, rolled down windows came a pleasant voice, which she traced to the face of a Saudi prince of a man dripping with the libido of a sexual pauper.

"Get bent!" she snarled.

"C'mon. You can't hate a guy for trying."

If her tone and word choice had not curbed his interest, the gesture of her hands did the trick. He rolled his window up and sped off squealing his new tires, shredding them into a pile of rubber.

Mona raised her hand up to her shoulder and wiped away an imaginary chip. It was a gesture that had become spiritual to her over time. She knew that any time she received someone else's bad energy she could make that gesture and rely on decades of self-acceptance and stick-to-it-tiveness to never fail her. Mona breathed in one more deep breath of self-indulgent solo time and softly put her phone back into its existential purpose of disturb mode. She laughed because she knew that antithetically if there were two modes and one was do not disturb the other was without question to inherently pester.

Immediately bells and whistles starting chiming. "Yeesh! Alright, alright already." She listened to a few voicemails to see what the supreme emergency was. She dialed Monique and talked while the phone was ringing. "Oh, what a surprise. Monique is having man trouble. I got ninety-nine problems and a..." Monique picked up and Mona just broke her inner dialogue with a greeting. "What's up Monique? I got your messages—"

"Mona! I did *not* see this coming. Shane just left me for his ex."

"Uh huh," Mona said with a knowing sigh.

"What are you—how could you know this was going to happen?"

"I told you he was hung up on his ex from day one. You changed the subject every single time I told you."

"You—but I just—I thought that would change!"

"Of course, you did. I can tell when

you're in denial—just like with that pastry chef. What was his name?"

"Chris? How could you bring up Chris right now?" Monique began crying into the phone.

"Oh now! Don't make me cry too. I love you—you know that, don't you?" Mona didn't want to hear her best friend crying, but she couldn't help but to have seen this whole thing coming. She had clearly told Monique more than five times that she needed to leave her boyfriend for someone who could return her affection. Monique was going through the twenties' codependent relationship struggles— the ones to which Mona simply didn't ever want to subscribe.

"Mona, you never have these issues, but you never date anyone. I've never seen you have one boyfriend in the three years I've known you." Monique paused and let out a few bursts of tears. "But, you're always happier than me..."

"Monique, don't compare yourself to other people. There is always a side you don't see. Everyone has their struggles—*everyone.*" Mona didn't have any regrets about being single. She knew all she needed was her ambition and goals. It disgusted her to think about a partner creeping in on her life and wrecking all the things that gave her peace of mind. But that didn't mean she never felt some tugs from her biological clock. It didn't mean a doubt didn't weasel its way into her mind now and again.

When the doubts came, she focused on her goals. She was already on year three of her degree and studying many upper level classes to go into clinical Psychiatry. She was fascinated with the neurology of the brain and the deeper topics within Psychotherapy.

"I feel so grateful to have a Psychiatrist for a friend..." Most people would have been saying this with some cynicism, but Monique was an opened book. She would make a terrible poker player.

"Here's my advice, Chica," Mona said. "Burn a candle. Turn the lights down. Breathe. I'm going to be there in the morning with breakfast."

"I'm only letting you in if you have waffles," Monique sobbed.

"Good night, sweetheart. There will definitely be waffles."

Chapter 3

Noel

Noel sat with his hands folded gently in his lap in the waiting area of Gate 3. A short bell sounded off on the overhead speakers and a pleasant female voice followed. "Welcome to Lincoln Airport. Now boarding for flight UA 3789 to Chicago. We are now boarding group A." Noel decided this was a good time to glance down at his ticket and figure out when he would be boarding. "That's swell I didn't even know there was a group D." He watched the whole room get onto the plane as he folded his arms. "Now boarding group D." Noel picked up his briefcase and wanted to wish back the time that he had lost waiting to board.

He crammed into the economy seats and noticed he had a middle seat. Most people would have noticed this before boarding, but he wasn't given to preparation for most things. He was stuck between two smelly gentlemen who were already having a heated debate about politics. He decided to call the heavy man John Candy and the slender man Steve Martin. As he placed his extra baggage in the overhead bin, he rolled his eyes. He then pardoned his way into the middle seat of the shouting match. "Don't mind me gentlemen."

"That's the problem with people like you! You think the world belongs to you!" Steve Martin shouted. He was drinking a green smoothie and wore workout clothes and a PeTA baseball cap. Meanwhile, John Candy was wearing a suit and tie. Noel already had them pegged as their proper wings of left and right.

"You don't care about the Constitution! You think that green smoothie is going to protect you if someone tries to steal your Fitbit?" Noel had to struggle to keep from laughing. This was where the real lawmaking happened, on a flight from nowhere to Chicago. What was going to get accomplished here? The heavy man pounded on Noel's shoulder. "What do you think, Mister?"

"I think it's too long a flight to talk about politics. I'd like to sleep the whole trip. Would either of you like to trade me seats so you can continue this debate without a middleman?"

"Me? Sit next to that pompous ass?" Steve Martin stuck out his bottom lip and folded his arms. Noel just rolled his eyes again and stuck in a pair of ear buds, which he cranked to full blast. He could see the men arguing out of his peripheral vision as the stewardess was at the front doing her display of emergency procedures. Noel pushed his seat back the standard ten-degree angle that the seat would allow. He wasn't used to falling asleep to heavy metal, but he hadn't been sleeping at all on the uncomfortable cabin bed. He woke up for a few minutes to some turbulence but otherwise slept the whole flight.

He arrived at the luggage conveyor and picked up his one huge suitcase which helped to weigh down the only free side of his body. He now carried a suitcase on one side and two carryon bags on the other. He looked like a one-man band with gigging equipment, but instead he had filled three pieces of luggage to capacity with clothes and over the counter medications. One bag was completely full of papers. He still couldn't figure if the papers in the carry on were in any way related to his life. All he knew was that he had shoved four manila folders full of lecture notes and xerox copies into a cramped tiny bag.

He stumbled back and forth left to right using his body to swing the luggage and propel his body to his father's car which was waiting outside the exit. He marveled at his father's ability to be there at just the right time. Other cars were getting motioned to move out of the way. There were officers in the road using walkie talkies to physically usher every single other vehicle out of the way, but his father sat there unnoticed. Noel had already determined that if it were him instead of his father people would have had no regard for innocent elderly misdirection. His father opened the car's boot.

"Do you feel as though you brought enough with you on your flight, Noel Roll?"

Noel sighed at the sound of his childhood nickname. "Yeah, it's good to see you too, father."

"Noel Roll, when have I been about formalities? You know yer mum and I are more than tickled to have you back, but you haven't even been gone for a full fortnight." His father closed the boot of the car.

"Isn't absence supposed to make the heart grow fonder?" Noel's brows lifted in a hopeful smile.

"I think it's fondue yer getting mixed up with. When you're not there my heart starts growing some delicious fondue for me and yer mum."

Noel never really understood his father's sense of humor. He raked a hand through his hair.

"Just get yer things in the boot and climb in, son. We're going to take you home, but not before you have some delicious dinner first."

"That sounds great, Dad. You know I didn't even have peanuts on the flight."

"I know, Noel Roll, you nay-ver eat or drink in the air. We brought you ten hours from overseas and thought you was going to dehydrate."

Noel walked over to the passenger-side door. "Dad, how have we sat here in the restricted area of the airport for so long without moving? It baffles me."

"I told them I was a doctor picking up a diplomat."

"And they believed you?"

Noel's father wiggled his eyes brows, dripping with charm. "Wouldn't you believe this face? Get in the car, Son. Its probably the accent. American's are suckers for my accent. Don't know why it doesn't have the same effect on your students…"

"Dad…you're incorrigible."

Chapter 4

Mona

Mona jolted up the steps to Monique's apartment. She was moving so fast that she almost charged into a slanky nerd who was meekly headed on his way down. She apologized, not because she was sorry, but because it was what people do when they almost plow someone over. Formalities like that were things that subconsciously annoyed Mona. She wanted to live in a world where people could be more objectivist. She stepped off the staircase and began walking down the narrow hallway until she heard Monique's dog barking wildly and scratching on the door. The noises were coming from so many different areas of the door that she knew the little Jack Russell was jumping and scratching like a dog-octopus hybrid.

Monique was wearing a purple onesie pajama outfit with dalmatian spots. She cracked the door and saw Mona long enough to close the door again and undo the chain lock. When Monique opened the door wide enough to accommodate her dog's ensuing bouncing, Mona knew well enough to guard the bag of waffles like a football player avoiding a fumble. She placed the breakfast bag on the table and walked to get a cold Red solo cup full of filtered water. Little puppy claws started swiping down her arms as Heather Dog pounced straight up to almost eye level. They had a habit of calling her Heather Dog because she shared a name with Monique's two-year-old cousin Heather. Monique had just the kind of Aunt and Uncle that didn't know her well enough to know that they were naming their firstborn after her dog.

"Oh, Holy Hell! I thought you would never get here! I'm dying. I didn't meditate AT ALL last night. I know I said I would, but I went straight for the vodka inside. I hit it *hard*, girl."

"How hard?" Mona bit her lip.

Monique scratched her head. "Not too bad, but I don't remember anything after I kicked on an old episode of Laugh-In."

"Laugh-In?" Mona snorted. "That show is terrible. Are you sure the show didn't make you high?"

"Ha! You're soooo funny, and that's exactly why I need you. I haven't laughed at anything since..."

Mona watched as the pain returned to her Monique's brown face, her full lips beginning to tremble. She pulled Monique in for a warm embrace. "Oh, Monique! Is that why you were watching Laugh-In? You poor thing! That's like snorting pixie sticks to clear a headache. The show was just made for people in the future to be baffled."

"I know, Mona. They made these faces like they were children and there was absolutely no intrinsic value to it." Monique did her best attempt at a naughty *oops* face and it was painful to see.

"Wow. Intrinsic? There's a word you don't use every day. No offense..."

"I know—" she started weeping. "It was the word of the day. Shane gave me a tear-off calendar full of them, girl."

"Oh man, we're going to have to burn that thing, aren't we?" Mona patted her bestie's back.

Monique wailed. And Mona let her—for about three long minutes—then she pulled away from their sloppy hug and she gripped Monique's big shoulders tightly enough to bruise. "It's out of your system. *He's* out of your system. What are you going to do sit here and feel sorry for yourself?"

"Yes?" Monique asked dabbing at her

eyes.

"Hell, no, girl! He wasn't worth it. He isn't worth another moment of your time or affection. Girl, these waffles are hot, and they are completely available. This is what we're going to do," Mona said, pulling out a chair at the dining table for her friend. "We're going to eat these delicious waffles with all the hot butter and syrup we want. Then we're going shopping. Retail therapy is exactly what you need. You know they're having a sale on lace panties at Versace?"

"Say what? Girl, you had me at the word sale." Monique inhaled half a waffle in about one second flat.

Monique wasn't exactly low maintenance, but she deserved patience after everything she was felling, whether Mona could completely empathize or not.

Once the shower was over, Mona did indulge in playing some up-tempo songs from her playlist and turning them up louder than anyone should. "Here—this is going to speed you up, try to do it in double time, like you're a spy in a movie that knows how to do everything quickly for a mission."

"Girl, I'ma forgive you for rushing me

because you brought me waffles..."

To pass the time Mona sat on the couch with Heather Dog and got on her phone. She began reading an article about a new medication and the receptors it affected despite so many treatment resistant patients. She was always doing all that she could to get an edge on her degree, even in the midst of distraction. "How we doing in there, Monique?" she said while scrolling to her email and sending herself a copy of the article for later.

"I am almost ready." Monique opened the bathroom door and stood there in her black bra and panties brushing her teeth. Mona wondered how in the hell this was all the progress made so far.

Instead of getting angry, she hopped off the couch and flitted to Monique's closet. "I'm going to pick out a dress. Is that okay?"

"Yes, but I haven't been to the gym in weeks, make sure it's on the left side for when I can't seem to disappear completely."

Mona sang the Radiohead song *How to Disappear Completely* in her mind knowing fully well that Monique just wouldn't get the reference. They had listened to the song together a hundred times, but Monique was never in the right place to catch references. "I'm not here, this isn't happening..."

"What did you say? I'm about to turn on the blow dryer."

"I'm singing, honey." The dryer kicked on and off from the next room. They had been semi-shouting as Mona rummaged through her closet, vetoing nearly every dress. She came across a black and red solid color dress that reminded her of art deco. It wasn't short, but it went down a little above the kneecap, and was one piece. She grabbed a lint brush from Monique's nightstand and removed all of Heather Dog's fur.

Monique laughed when she watched Mona hang the dress on the opened bathroom door. "Thanks! I love this one. Knew you would pick it." Monique was applying beautiful false lashes, the kind Mona never had time for. Her contacts were trouble enough.

After another fifteen minutes, Monique emerged from the bathroom looking like a million bucks. "I can't believe you ever lowered yourself to date that piece of garbage. You are *so hot*! Look in the mirror for God sakes."

Monique was full-figured, nowhere as athletic as Mona, but she had the hour-glass figure of a Kardashian and didn't seem to know it. "I just don't see what you do, Mona. I'm just Monique from Indiana in a dress that is way prettier than I am."

"Shut the front door. Girl, you make that dress. You look great. We're going, now. That was record time...*48 minutes 20 seconds.* Get your black purse."

Monique dropped some food in Heather Dog's bowl and refilled the water right before she set up the childproof gate to keep Heather Dog in the laundry room. She walked toward the door and Heather Dog jumped right over the gate.

"I don't know why I try!"

Both girls giggled as Monique grabbed a waffle for the road.

Chapter 5

Noel

Noel's father, Harry, emerged from the kitchen, which just looked like a light at the end of a tunnel, because his parents kept their house unnaturally dark. He was holding two bowls of shepherd's pie. The form with which he was holding them let Noel know they were lukewarm instead of piping hot.

Noel sighed but decided against offering complaint. There was no point.

His mother, Patricia, wobbled into the cave of a living room with an apron on. "Well, Noel Roll, doesn't dinner smell nice?"

Noel dutifully gathered the lukewarm bowl in his hands and made a show of enjoying a morsel. "It's got to be some of the best you've made, mum. I'm just happy to see you."

"Well, I hope you eat the lot of it because we have to make our way downtown."

"Oh no, Mum? I can't...no...I'm just exhausted."

"I won't hear any more of it. Greta is coming over tonight with her daughter and she can't have a baby shower because she doesn't have any friends. Her daughter is just backward, son. She barely speaks English. Greta got custody of her from Germany when she was sixteen, and now she's eighteen and having a baby. What was her name? Oh yeah, Martha. Martha is so awkward. I've got to go downtown and get her some skivvies. It's the only thing I can afford frankly and there is a sale."

"Do you really think that is appropriate for a baby shower? You know most people buy something for the baby, Mum?"

"I already have the stroller that we used for you, Noel Roll. We had given it to your Aunt Vera many years ago, and she brought it back when I told her about this. But Martha is so depressed. The boy that got her pregnant flew back to Cambodia, I think it was, and Greta is trying to get her to move on. There's nothing that helps a woman get over her ex like fancy underwear."

The whole thing sounded absurd. "Maybe that is why I just don't have a woman. I doubt I will ever understand them."

His dad finally stopped eating long enough to say his piece. "I hear you *lout* and *clear*, Noel Roll. Nothing helps a man like a few pints of ale." Noel felt proud that in his last three years of being single he hadn't had to give in to a single drinking session with his buddies or his father.

Shopping with Mum suddenly sounded like a godsend. "I'll drive you anywhere you like, Mum."

"OH, NOEL ROLL!!! I'm so happy. You are the best son ever. Now, you're going to shave, aren't you?"

Noel felt his face and noticed that he had neglected his face for weeks. In place of a smooth, gentle, rounded jawline he had a scruffy salt and pepper mess. "You know, Mum, I promised I would help you, but I didn't say I was going to be responsible about it. I am my father's son, and he taught me only to shave for job interviews and bachelor parties." Noel ran his hand through his hair and noticed the dark jet-black shine was only prominent from the excess oil. Airplanes, though sanitary were always a place to collect a disheveled appearance. "It's good 'nuff for gov'ment work."

"Where do you get these Americanisms?"

"Oh, Mum, they're called colloquialisms."

"Now what in the Dickens makes you think I will remember that?"

"Dickens. I wonder if that is considered a colloquialism—it's got to be about Charles Dickens hasn't it?"

"I don't know. Don't care. You think too much. If you're going like that, we can leave in a few minutes—all I need to do is spray some perfume. "

Harry chimed in again. "Noel, you are a great son. You always say you wish you had made more money, but it isn't about that. It's about how much you drop everything to help your mother and I."

Noel lived for those times that his dad was serious. He laughed inside about how doing something so mundane and surreal as driving his mother downtown to buy underwear for the neighborhood girl was one of the grandest achievements of his life. Maybe this was his purpose after all. It had proven too illusive to discover a better purpose on his sojourn out of town.

Pretty soon they were on the road and Noel could care less that his suitcase and carryon's lay in the front doorway.

His mother made light conversation the whole way telling him he needed to find a good woman. It was great that on top of his nagging single life misery, he got the added plus of having his mother berate him about his choices. And, it was just like the elderly to act like being single was his choice—as if he could just put some Brylcreem in his hair and throw on some Stetson and all the women would be lined up for him to choose one, as they stood there all trim, smoking cigarettes like an old-fashioned Zigfried follies show.

He just made light of the whole situation and began to do something he hadn't done for a long decade. He began to think deeply about how bad it all could be. He didn't know why he was doing this, but it seemed to feel good inside. He realized some people don't even have a relationship with their parents, much less a good job and a college education. And, somewhere under his damaged vision of his self was the esteem to be glad he was one of the brightest Physicists in his field. He started reminding himself of how he stood out at graduation with his thesis on the conditions needed for the energy and environment to split matter and reproduce particles. It was all theoretical since the conditions would never be present, but he was able to discover that under the right laboratory settings and with the proper nuclear and atomic disruptions—matter could be replicated. As far as it existed in his mind— he could simply make two hydrogen atoms out of one, but the price was outstanding, and no one would ever want to see such a thing at least in his lifetime.

SCREEETCH! He had to slam on his brakes because someone was trying to cut him off on the highway. "SHIT!"

"Noel Roll! Do you have to use locker room talk around your mother?"

"Sorry, Mum. It just slipped out. I don't think it's anything you haven't heard before. After all, I probably learned it from you and Dad."

"Just be careful and get us to the store—there are probably women from all over town trying to—OUCH! My back!"

"What's wrong? Do you want me to take us back home?"

"No, I'm ok—I'm just having one of those fits again. Getting in the car is too much strain. I'm sure it will stop by the time we get there."

"Just let me know, the GPS says we're ten minutes away." He glanced back up to the road from the cell phone sitting in his lap.

"You're not using that map on your phone? Noel Roll! On your lap of all things! I'd like to get there in one piece, even if my whole body is aching."

"Mom. I don't exactly go to Versace all the time. I've never been there. What did you think, that I was going to stick my finger in the air and head west?"

"You are just like your father, but I haven't killed him yet. Just watch the road, and I'll direct you the rest of the way. Put that phone away. Then I can quit worrying about an accident killing us both."

It was an adventure just to find parking, but when they finally did, Noel jumped out and stepped up to the sidewalk to open his mother's door. She began to step out of the car and began wincing in pain.

"I can't handle it—it's like a rope is tied to my back and a horse is riding in the other direction. Noel Roll. You're going to have to go buy these for me."

"Mum! I've got to protest!" This is the absolute worst thing that could have happened. He half wondered if drinking with his dad's crusty friends would have been better.

"You simply must. We didn't come here for nothing." Mum was wearing her resolute face, the one that made her look mildly like Winston Churchill.

Noel's brow twitched. "How am I going to know what you were going to buy?"

"They have a whole bunch of zebra print and polka dots. Just buy three of those in any order. I don't care what color. I wrote the size on this notecard. You know, something sexy, Lad."

"I simply can't believe this is happening. How do I get myself into these predicaments? Mum... You owe me. You are not making us sing carols at Christmas. No going around the neighborhood. Not after this."

"Noel Roll! You really drive a hard bargain. You have been trying to get me to cancel that every year since you were a little lad. If you would just lighten up, you wouldn't have so much trouble finding a good woman!"

"Mother. I love you." He shut the door and she continued talking as if he could hear her outside the car window. He couldn't and he was grateful.

The walk to the store was bugging him. He was talking to himself and he rarely did that. He was saying things like, "Stupid Christmas carols. None of us can carry a tune in a bucket.

The neighbors have a difficult time."

Chapter 6

Mona

Mona and Monique made their way over every inch of the store. Monique was getting tired and she leaned on a small rack of shirts, but her hungover body was a little too much for the skimpy fixture. The whole rack fell over, Monique with it.

Mona laughed out loud. "Didn't know it wouldn't support you?" Mona laughed so loudly kids began laughing with her as they walked by. "Don't worry, Monique. These shirts were meant to be folded anyway. That rack isn't worth a dime." Mona began picking up the shirts and folding them one by one.

"Ow," Monique rubbed her elbow and joined right into the laughing. She only stopped long enough to point a serious finger at one of the children. "If I see this on Instagram I will cut you."

Mona shook her head. She continued to pick up shirts and fold them neatly when a man who was clearly talking to himself wandered over to her. "Excuse me, *Miss. Where do you keep your panties?*"

Mona couldn't help herself. "Usually

under my clothes," she quipped. She was aware
he thought she worked there, but she was not
patient enough to deal with him.

"Er...right...sorry. What I mean was I
need some size eight panties, they're on sale."

Mona looked the man up and down. "I'd
say you are an eleven."

"Oh no!" He turned purple. "They're not
for me. The nerve. I'm buying them for a
teenage girl! Oh wait, that sounded
strange...didn't it? My mother told me to buy
them for a neighborhood girl."

Monique and Mona laughed out loud.

"Oh, bloody hell! You've found me out
then. I was lying before. They're for me. Can you
just point me in the right direction?"

Monique spoke up and decided to end
the whole thing before he had a meltdown. "Sir,
the panties are right behind you in that bin."

He turned around and grumbled as he
walked toward the underwear.

"And sir!" Monique finished as the
European man looked back at her. "My friend
doesn't work here and neither do I. You should
practice being more observant."

The man's face turned from purple to red. He began digging through the pile haphazardly until he found what he needed.

"Strange one, huh?" Mona whispered to Monique.

"Yeah. Poor dude. He looks more stressed than I am," her bestie answered.

Chapter 7

Noel

When Noel got back in the car, he practically threw the bag into his mother's lap.

"Noel, Love, is something wrong?"

"Nothing Mum. Let's just leave it at that. Those are the ones you asked for."

"Well you are right." She spun the undergarments in her hands. "You picked the right ones out and everything."

"Yes. But at what cost?" Noel hung his head for a moment.

"What does that mean? Do you have a fever? You're turning colors, Lad." His mum reached over to feel his forehead, but he pulled away from her reach.

"I'm fine. Let's just go home. I need to take my bags to my apartment. It has been great catching up with you and Dad, but I'm exhausted." Noel put the car in gear.

"We've loved every moment. When do you go back to work?"

"I'm off for a month. I guess I'm going to start writing that book I always wanted to write." At the notion, Noel smiled. A little.

"That sounds great! Now I hope you'll come visit next week."

"When do I not? I have no friends except for Ricardo, and he won't be back for a week."

"I hope you don't get depressed without work. It is so easy for someone to get depressed without work and being single." Noel's mother sucked her teeth.

"Yes, Mother. I heard. I need a good woman. The way I'm scaring them off—I don't think I have a chance in hell, though."

"That's just not true."

They drove home in silence; Noel got home and hugged his father before hurrying into his car which he had left in front of their house for the last month.

#

Noel had a hell of a week. He felt like he had put on three pounds. Every day was takeout food and sitting on his couch, just to repeat the process the week after. He finished just a small portion of a work of fiction he had started but spent nearly all the time binge watching Netflix series and reality television. He had left his physics work where it belonged—in his laboratory room. His living room was starting to get messy. If he was honest, the living room was beginning to smell. There were open books and wadded up newspapers lining the floor. Each day he made a note to clean the next day, but he never actually did it until one of the piles on the floor moved and he was frightened something might be living beneath it.

He turned on a sad slow song about unrequited love and began mopping the kitchen. Two hours later he had listened to a playlist of all the sad songs in history while he finally got his apartment halfway presentable. The smell was gone, and that alone was a triumph.

He sat down and began typing and finished two sentences before starting to fall asleep at his keyboard. It was three p.m. and he wasn't someone accustomed to napping so early in the day. What did it say about his fiction writing prowess that his own novel was causing him to dose off?

Regardless, Noel fell asleep. In his most vivid dreams, he was, unfortunately, being attacked by a dog. It was the kind of dream where he could feel pain as if it were real, and when he was about to wake up, he felt like someone was holding him down. He often had bouts with sleep paralysis, but he was so used to it he just woke up finally and shook his head. He poured a dark cup of coffee at four thirty and decided to go to the gym.

He dialed Ricardo handsfree while he was driving but got his voicemail message and hung up. It had taken him a half hour to get all the things he needed for the gym, toiletries and junk. As he pulled up to the gym, he noticed a huge firetruck sitting outside. He pulled up to park in the huge parking lot but was blocked by construction cones. He noticed the doorway was singed and police tape draped around the door. He wondered how long his gym had been burned. He pulled into the only free parking space and dialed the gym customer service. The young woman explained that there had been a fire two days ago, and Noel pondered how anyone could start a fire in a gym. He drove to the nearest park with a walking track and he wandered to the concrete section made for track stars and serious runners. He just paced around the track for twenty laps until the sun went down as people ran past him time after time. He got back into the car and tried calling Ricardo again.

"Hey buddy! I'm going to be home tomorrow! Let's meet up and go to the gym!"

Ricardo had picked up and answered cheerfully.

"You wouldn't believe it, but the gym actually caught fire. It's going to be closed for a week, at least."

"What did you do, run so fast it started sparks on the treadmill?" Ricardo chuckled at his own joke.

"Ha! Yeah, I was like the Flash. No, seriously, one of the workers lit a cigarette in the sauna and left it there to make out with a girl in the steam room."

"Where do guys get all this action? He must have been a young buck. I haven't kissed a woman for months."

"Tell me about it. I'm going on three years."

"Wow. Noel. We gotta get you—"

"Yeah, yeah, you gotta get me laid. I should get a dollar every time someone says that."

"Then you could buy a prostitute."

"Not that desperate yet."

"I hear that. ...They're never as hot as in the movies anyway."

Noel wrinkled his lip in disgust.

"Hey, listen, I'm at the airport," Ricardo continued. "This has been a wonderful vacay. I'm really gonna miss Greece, but anyway, I gotta let you go. We'll meet up tomorrow and we'll go to the horse track."

"Yeah. Anything's better than getting fat on the couch."

"Shut up, Man. I wish I had your metabolism. But I'll see you soon."

"Later."

Noel pressed the small red button on his steering wheel that ended the call. It saddened him that time with Ricardo was the only thing he had to look forward to. The horse track was something Ricardo loved, and Noel just suffered the trips.

He was driving back to his office and a car came plowing past him in the left lane. He had to swerve off of the road onto the shoulder to avoid getting hit, and, noticing a construction sign blocking his path, his only remaining option was to make a swift right turn into a shopping plaza, so he flipped his signal on as quickly as possible and headed into the parking lot.

Was it a full moon or something? Where could anyone possibly have to be that they'd risk hitting another person along the way?

Noel sighed. When he looked up at the shopping center, he saw two beautiful older women walking into a hair salon and began thinking deeply about his dating problems. At what age was it time to really give up, he wondered. He had completely spaced out and when he returned to reality, the women had caught him staring. Of course, he'd only started checking them out. Now he was more focused on his troubles than on their well-aging bodies.

He could hear them through his cracked passenger window saying, "Geez. Take a picture. Creep." His face grew hot. He pulled over in between some white lines and parked to gather his thoughts. "I can't go on like this," he said to himself. "It's driving me insane." After, he spoke aloud he questioned his own sanity and turned up a song on the satellite radio. It must have been fate. *All By Myself* by Eric Carmen filled his ears and his soul.

He felt like life was playing some cosmic joke on him. As the song ended, a radio DJ offered one of the few ads on this channel, saying "Tired of living with loneliness, anxiety and depression? Get therapy. Our counsellors will help you get on your A game. Jessica Millhouse, LSW, Brain Power Workshop. Book your spot today!"

"Why not?" Noel said aloud. After the month he'd had, anything was worth a try. He brought up his GPS and thought there must be some mistake when Mrs. Millhouse's office was in this very plaza. Ordinarily, Noel wasn't much for believing in signs, but the sun was shining only on the one office building as he gaped at it. It was as if heaven was trying to tell him something. He could almost hear a chorus of angels singing.

Taking a chance, he walked in and stopped in front of the receptionist. The room smelled like three or four kinds of aromatherapy and the furniture was perfectly matched to the interior which had been professionally decorated. He felt like he was in an upscale massage parlor thanks to the paintings of peaceful landscapes, mostly vast and serene vistas of calm waters and smooth coastlines. "Oh, no! I can't do this. I'm sorry for taking up your time, ma'am." Noel started to turn on his heel.

"Sir, you haven't said anything yet." The woman was wearing dangling earrings and her eyes wrinkled up when she smiled.

Noel frowned at her. "It's just...I have to go this is not right for me. This was a mistake."

"Your first time huh?" she arched a brow. "Therapy is for weirdo's and the lonely kid who draws demented pictures in class, am I right?" She pursed her lips.

"Uh, yeah. How did you know?" Noel took a tentative step closer to her.

"Well, you are stepping in here with the apprehension of someone skydiving for the first time." She had one of the prettiest faces he had ever seen. Her cheeks were full, her eyes bright. He went through the top ten most beautiful women he had ever met and then remembered number one was the woman who he'd mistaken as a store clerk at Versace. The one who guessed he could use a size eleven thong.

She was petite, with auburn hair with crazy shine, and bright, fierce eyes, as if you could stick her in your pocket, but she'd bite you for trying. She'd bite you—but you might enjoy it.

Her friend was hot, too, he remembered, but a little high maintenance and not really his type.

"Why didn't I get her name?" He said out

loud. Not only did the memory make him miserable, but now he was also terrified that his verbal filter had stopped working.

"Oh! What? This sounds like a juicy story! Whose name is that, Sir?" The receptionist leaned in with a look so eager, she might as well pop some popcorn while she was at it.

"Oh, I don't know why I said that out loud." Noel scratched his head awkwardly. "It's just that you are beautiful, and I'm not coming on to you, I promise, but I can't help myself. I have been single for a long time—"

The receptionist batted her lashes, clearly flattered. "Sir, I'm definitely not being rude, but you can see I have a ring..." She did. And when she held it up, it caught the light and looked expensive.

Noel cleared his throat and loosened the collar of his shirt. "No, it's not that. You just— you reminded me of someone—someone who I have a feeling might have been special. I guess—I guess I am saying I *definitely* need to talk to a therapist. I talked to the most beautiful woman in my life and she must have thought I was a fool yesterday. I don't know why I screwed it up so badly..."

"No, I see. This isn't that rare of a problem, Sir. Men in the prime of life start second guessing themselves all the time after being single for an extended time. It happens to women, too. You came to the right place. Jessica is an outspoken life coach for businessmen, teachers, and athletes alike who need to learn skills to cope with relationships and even loneliness issues."

Noel lifted his brows in surprise. "It's funny you said teachers. I happen to teach physics…"

"You see, what is happening, Sir? You have a very exciting life, and now you are talking a little about yourself, and it peaks someone's interest. I'm sure you have just developed some coping habits over time that have led you to believe you aren't as diverse and spontaneous. The self-esteem can be damaged by not having the tools to create good mental habits. This isn't a life ending problem." The receptionist nodded encouragingly. She certainly had confidence in spades.

"It's funny you say it that way, because it feels like life isn't going anywhere for me. I'm in idle. I feel stagnant." Just then he looked to the waiting room and saw an older woman who was looking at him with judgment. "I guess this isn't the place to talk about my problems. Well it is, but not the waiting room. I should probably see the therapist right away."

The young woman laughed. "Therapy isn't like meeting with a car mechanic. You don't bring your brain in and get it looked at. We set up an appointment when it is convenient for you and you come back and have a quiet session with the therapist. Can I set you up an appointment? Our first open session is next week."

"I have to think about it. I just don't know." He turned around and was about to head outside when he saw yet another attractive woman come out of the back room and head for the door. "Let me get the door for you!" He rushed in front of her and swung the door open only to swing the door right into the path of an elderly man who almost fell down on the sidewalk outside. "I'm so sorry, Sir." The lady laughed at him and he quickly went back to the receptionist's desk. "On second thought. I'll see the therapist next week. Should I spell my last name for you?"

In the end, she handed him a card which was already filled out. He marveled at her level of intelligence and intuition for being someone who just made appointments and he begrudgingly made his way home.

#

The next morning, Ricardo picked Noel up in front of his apartment building. Ricardo was wearing the same goofy outfit from his vacation with the look of a Cuban revolutionary in the nineteen sixties. It was perfect attire for the racetrack. "Wow, Ricardo. You really look the part."

"You like it? I went all in for this one. I bought this for my vacation, and it just kinda grew on me." He adjusted to the dark shades on his nose.

Noel was fully amused by the getup since Ricardo had been the type to dress rather stylishly when they went on adventures. It was nothing abnormal for Noel to see him in a blazer and slacks with an expensive gold watch. The watch was missing, and Noel had to say something. "What happened to your watch?"

"I'm not proud of this, buddy, but I had to hock it."

"'Hock' it? I'm sorry I don't know what that means."

"I forget sometimes you didn't grow up here. Well, I sold it to a pawn shop." Ricardo shrugged. "I was getting low on cash after going to the casino."

"Gambling? When did you start this?"

"I don't know—Honestly, I picked up the habit last month. I went into a casino for the first time and won--turned a hundred bucks into three thousand. Then, over the course of two weeks I gambled away all but five hundred of it."

Noel stopped in his tracks. "I mean, we used to go to the horse track once a year, and now you're jumping off your airplane and going straight to the track? Maybe we need to turn around."

Ricardo whirled to face him. "No. I got a friend who tells me how to win at the track. It's fool proof. He gave me this list of horses and they are sure to win." Ricardo smirked.

"Oye. This sounds like a total red flag, Man."

Ricardo only winked. "Let's do this. Drinks are on me once we get there."

So, after a short drive, they walked in as normal and began placing their bets on the horses. Each bet, Ricardo was making a higher gamble than the last. He had a list of ten horses, and he placed bets on the first nine races. Noel placed a few two-dollar bets, but Ricardo had bet the whole illustrious five hundred he had on all nine horses. The two of them screamed and yelled while nearly each horse on the list won their races bringing Ricardo to a huge sum of winnings. He waited till right before the tenth race to go cash in all the tickets. A man in the cashier's office tallied up his winnings and hesitated before giving him the money. "Sir. It looks like you got extremely lucky." The cashier was very polite and reassuring.

"Yep. I just have a knack for it." Ricardo was drooling over the money.

"Well, sir. Surely you read our policy about winnings over five thousand?"

Ricardo frowned. "No, I actually didn't."

"Yes, it's in the fine print at the bottom of the brochure, but if you win more than five thousand in any given day—there is no question about it, but you must wait two hours to get a signed check from the horse track. It is just our policy. A lot of people will come and cash in each ticket throughout the day, but you have brought them all at the same time tonight."

"Oh. I'm happy to win, but I was going to

place a bet on the last race."

"I'm sorry, Sir." The cashier got on the phone. "My manager says that we will give you the check in one hour, but that won't be in time for the race."

Ricardo pulled Noel out of the line and cornered him against a wall. "Noel, you saw what happened. They zapped me. I got no money. You're going to have to float me this one. We'll pick up the money after the race and I'll pay you back."

"I can't argue—we both saw all of your horses win the race. I'm sure your list is good." What else could he say?

"Hey, keep it down. They could hear you." Ricardo was more moody than usual, but then it had been an emotional day.

"You're right. Well, this is the money in my account for my therapy sessions. I have to pay them tomorrow. I've got two-fifty."

"That's all you got? Where's all your money?" Noel tried to ignore it when some spittle flew from Ricardo's lips.

"I've got money in savings, and I donated a large portion to my retirement this week, but the check from the lectures in Nebraska won't be in until Friday, and it's more substantial than what you would think."

Ricardo's wide eyes grew wild. "They paid you more than they pay me?"

"Well, I wasn't supposed to tell you, but they gave me a few thousand more?" Noel winced.

"How much? Tell me!"

Noel told him the sum and Ricardo threw his hat on the ground. "Noel. You got to give me that two hundred and fifty, this is a sure thing. It's going to win us a fortune. And it would appear you owe me! I'm the one that got you the gig filling in for me."

"Horse racing is never a sure thing, but your guy hasn't been wrong before." Noel sighed. He hated seeing Ricardo this way. "I'll give you the money. But you have to pay me back before three p.m. tomorrow."

The joy returned to Ricardo's face. "I'm going to my bank first thing in the morning and cash the check."

Noel went to the ATM and drew enough money to place the bet, and they made their final wager of the night.

Like clockwork the horse won. Noel was flabbergasted when he saw the check for a final total of eighteen thousand, five hundred, and forty-six bucks. But something Ricardo said earlier was weighing on him, "So, you don't have any money at all, Ricardo? You're really broke?"

"Hey, you just saw—I got a check for eighteen thousand, and I'm giving you three thou for your bet. What are you grinding me for?" Ricardo waved Noel off as they walked toward the car.

"Buddy. It's me." Noel moved in front of his friend, blocking his path. "You must have gambled a lot more if you only had five hundred dollars today. Look at me, Ricky. Look at me." Ricardo looked at Noel, and only then did he continue to speak in an even and serious tone. "You have to *promise* me you aren't going to gamble any more. You have kids. If I catch you gambling again—you have to go, get help."

"Geez. If you put it that way..." Ricardo sighed. "I guess I'm going to get help anyway. Someone who spends all their money from a habit they picked up a month ago, needs to stop it fast, but I'm cashing this check in the morning and paying you the money so you can go to your precious therapy sessions."

Noel smiled. "I know. It sounds weird. Therapy. But I can't be myself around women anymore. They are all distracting me. My behavior is out of control. I don't even feel human anymore. How am I supposed to date when I'm constantly giving off creeper vibes?"

Ricardo patted his friend on the back. "Hey, Noel, I don't think it's so weird to get therapy. You're a good looking and successful guy. There's got to be something wrong with your brain up there if you can't find someone after the Guinness World's Record of three years of being single."

"Hey. Someone's been single longer than that, but I can assure you they probably have a therapist and a psychiatrist working around the clock."

"That's true," Ricardo laughed. "Let me take you home and then I'll see you in the morning."

The track had never been Noel's favorite place in the world, but after the highs and lows of the eventful day, he had to admit, he was feeling cautiously optimistic for a change.

Chapter 8

Mona

Mona woke up in her apartment. She yawned, stretched, and reached to turn on her bedside lamp. Her room was conspicuously tidy. Every surface gleamed with the sort of clean you could eat from. Every little thing sat in its designated place. It was as if a maid service came in every day and cleaned up. Order brought Mona comfort. Order brought her a sense of peace and pride.

A huge fan of meditation, she slipped into her house shoes and turned on her morning "Empowerment of the Mind" collection. The mantras began playing. They weren't the run of the mill self-empowerment mantras, either. No, Sir. Instead they focused on unlocking personal achievements and taking the world by storm. After all, she saw herself as a tower of success and not someone who needed the paltry self-esteem boost. It was "business" esteem she needed, and her audio files were full of business-themed inspiration.

She knew she didn't have the warm and cuddly bedside manner many psychologists did. She also knew that it irked people and sometimes got her into trouble, but she felt like her completely objectivist approach would be exactly what set her apart. Her ability to fix people rather than heal people would make her less of a patsy. It was picking herself up by her own bootstraps that got her to where she was, and she felt others should be capable of the same, even if they just needed a firm boost.

She mused about how she had easily taken her friend from zero to autopilot. In Mona's mind—her ability in the social world came from being able to put people back in charge of their own destiny. She could live her life knowing that her friends and acquaintances were off in the distance performing in a mechanical sense. They were doing things much like little clocks she had put together from little pieces.

She took an invigorating shower and headed off to class. Today was the big day that she would be assigned an internship. Even though most of her studies were in the biological workings of the brain, this was a class devoted purely to clinical therapy. The Psychiatrist would know how to throw pills at the mentally defeated, but classes like these would reveal the powers of Cognitive Behavioral Therapy.

She was seated in class when she noticed today was quiet compared to other days. Most of the students were focused on finding out where they would be rather than the usual morning where the professor had to come and talk everyone down from catching up from the weekend. Faces were looking forward and the students were wearing lab coats. She was assigned her spot with a local clinical therapist along with two other students. Her team consisted of herself, Malcolm Theroux, and Lisa "Kitty" White. Malcolm was biracial and spoke with absolute deep throated authority, as if he had caught a catfish in his voice box, and Kitty was the average, sorority girl airhead. Mona raged inside that she got the two most eccentric characters in the class. It would be distracting, and Mona had no time for that. The conversation would be so "cutesy" and based around references to the TV show Scrubs which she had always seen Malcolm and Kitty talking about together before class.

Mona immediately offered to be group leader which meant contacting the therapist's office and virtually shoving the University's foot in the door. Mona liked the thought of calling a local therapist's office and bossing around their staff until she and her team obtained their day of observation. The therapists had already cornered themselves into a contract with the University and it was something none of the local therapists had wanted to do. It was a reluctant way of adding a stipend onto their business. The students would take a simple session with a client and observe it from a room down the hall. It was broadcast over Bluetooth from a camera in the therapy room and the students would be able to speak about every aspect of the session. It was as real-world as student work could get.

Mona took the paperwork and left class with a feeling of superiority. It was something that made her even more sure of herself, and she lived for moments like these. She made sure not to say anything condescending to her classmates on her way out. If their morale stayed high, she wouldn't need to put them in their places.

After she went home—she discarded her lab coat and went to the gym for a three-hour power workout. Afterwards, she settled into the local coffee shop and put on a wireless ear bud as she drank some decaf espresso and called the local therapist with her script. She had already decided she would probably go off script because if anyone could improvise it would be her. The receptionist answered, "Brainworks. How can we make your life better?"

"Hello, this is Mona Lawson from the University of Illinois in Chicago. Our clinical

Psychology students are starting their yearly internships—"

"Miss Lawson, was it? Please hold." There was immediate hold music.

Mona loathed hold music...

Chapter 9

Noel

Noel was rushing through his day, making up for yet another morning of sleeping in like a frat boy. His face was covered in a beard which would never grow right. His clothes smelled like his bed sheets, which hadn't been washed in weeks. It wasn't a terribly bad smell, but it was musky, for sure. He called Ricardo for the twelfth time and left a stern message, "I have to call the therapist right now. I DON'T want to talk to my parents because I haven't borrowed money for a decade—" Just as he was on his tirade, a call patched through from Ricardo.

"Hey, Noel. Buddy. I went to the bank and they said that since I had never cashed a check that large, they had to put a two day hold on it. I'm so sorry to let you down."

Noel sighed deeply. "What can I do, Ricardo? I have no choice but to call the therapist and give up these meetings. I never wanted to do them in the first place, and it's not like I'm hard up for cash. I could dip into my savings if I had to, but not for some stupid shrink. You tried. Just give me the money when you can. No hard feelings." Noel hung up feeling defeated.

Noel was dreading making this call. He felt like a proper fool. He knew the receptionist would recognize him as the confounded British man with relationship issues. He had hoped to blend in as just another client, but now he would be known forever as the indecisive man who couldn't handle making a simple decision.

When he finally dialed the number, he was instantly put on hold. It gave him plenty of time to wallow in his ineptitude.

"Thank you for holding, this is Jessica Millhouse how may I be of service?"

Noel was very happy to hear that the receptionist wasn't answering today. But he found it intimidating that he had to speak with the actual therapist. "Er, Mrs. Millhouse, this is Noel Kensington. I am a new client, and it I have the terrible news that I must cancel my first session. I had financial difficulty—I don't know why I'm going into such detail, but story short, I do regret that I must cancel my sessions."

"Well Mr. Kensington," said the therapist in a very energized voice, "You see, you caught me at a very significant moment. I am in a special position to offer your first month free if you will consent to additional monitoring from my interns. You won't even know they are there, it is done by video, but this means our sessions together won't be as private as usual. You'd be assisting in training the next generation of therapists."

That's just what Noel needed, a larger audience to look foolish for. "I don't know that kind of—"

"Mr. Kensington. The sessions would be absolutely free. I am begging you to help the field of Psychiatry. These people need this experience to grow and help save people in very desperate situations."

He could tell by the tension in her voice that she really wanted him to say yes. "Well, I'm a professor myself. When you put it that way...? I guess I could take a discount to help save the world."

"Yes! Mr. Kensington, you won't regret this. Just come into your session and my receptionist will help you sign the waiver. All that it means is that my interns will monitor a couple of sessions from a room down the hallway. They won't interact with you, and the sessions will be confidential. They know better than to disclose to anyone what they hear."

"Ok. I guess. Sounds good to me."

"Please come in for your session and be prepared to tackle your issues. You are going to get through this. You have the power."

"Well, that's great. I feel very good already. I think you are going to be a help."

"Thank you. See you Thursday."

Mona

"Thank you for holding, Ms. Lawson. I've got great news for you and the other interns," Mrs. Millhouse said over the phone. "Your first session is scheduled for Thursday."

Mona had the sinking feeling that something had gone on while she was on hold, but it didn't matter. What mattered was getting this internship. "Okay, wonderful. My team will see you Thursday when you open your doors."

"Have a great day." The therapist hung up in what seemed like a hurry, leaving Mona alone to scratch her head.

Chapter 10

Mona

Mona sat in a small room with nothing but three chairs and a computer screen. Her classmates were using the time to brown nose Mrs. Millhouse into giving them letters of recommendation, but Mona knew it was in the bag. She felt like it was a routine day in her life. It wasn't the hardest of all classes, but she sat with good posture and couldn't wait to finish this project.

Pretty soon her teammates came back to their respective chairs each with snacks and coffee. "See Mona, you should have come with us. We got all kinds of treats." Malcolm croaked. Mona hoped he wouldn't say much else because the room was not acoustic enough to contain the booming alto.

"I'm not big on sweets, Malcolm. By the way, Kitty, I think you were just trying to impress Mrs. Millhouse by taking the client aside and having a personal chat. I'm not trying to be rude, but the last thing a patient needs is a student poking into their affairs."

Kitty spoke up, "You know what I think, Mona? I think people who have to constantly say they aren't trying to be rude, absolutely are trying to be rude. Mind your business.”

“Uh, ladies, Malcolm cut in loudly if not awkwardly. “We’re supposed to be quiet in here. I can see the second patient of the day on camera now. Says here his name is Noel Kensington, and he’s a physics professor with relationship and anxiety issues. This ought to be good, no?”

Mona stared daggers at Kitty until the sorority gal rolled her eyes and scooted closer to the feed to watch.

Mona watched the first few minutes of pleasantries unfold as Mrs. Millhouse introduced herself and got a background workup on Noel. It was interesting to get into the details of someone else’s life. The picture on the screen wasn’t zoomed-in enough to show this patient’s face clearly, but Mona couldn’t help but think his voice was recognizable.

She didn’t want to chase the notion in her head because you could be suspended from the program for being part of a study on anyone you could possibly know. It constituted a conflict of interest. Anyway, if she really knew the man called Noel, she’d have more easily remembered him.

She and the team listened and wrote

down their notes about body language and verbal cues. Mona smirked when she notices all three interns scratched down the word: fidgety. He was constantly moving, the poor soul. He kept saying his patented catch phrase, "Come again?"

Then, Mrs. Millhouse asked the question, "What are you really here for? What is the number one thing you can't get off your mind?"

Noel took a second and he looked like a skydiver about to leap from a plane.

Then, he began to cry. "I've been single for so long—it's depressing. Any time I meet a beautiful woman I become mush, nonsensical mush. OR, if it isn't all about me being a complete turn off—I do something stupid and it is miles away from charming. I can give you the perfect example. I can't stop thinking about the biggest buffoonery I've had lately. This woman," Noel wiped some tears on his sleeve, "was a ten! She was confident and attractive, and I liked everything about her. She just looked like one of those people who could fascinate you every day for a lifetime. But from the moment we met, it was me nonstop digging my own grave. And!" Noel laughed bitterly, "The more I screwed up, the more I liked her! But," he swallowed, "I saw her at Versace, the one on Main, and I mistook her for a store clerk, and I don't think she or her gal pal liked that. I made a total arse of myself?"

"Take your time," Mrs. Millhouse said, "Sometimes it is as simple as compartmentalizing what you are truly trying to say.

"Poor dweeb," Kitty remarked.

Malcom shook his head with pity, then sat up straighter in his seat. "Even I have a better rapport with the ladies than this guy."

Mona just froze. Oh. *No.* This is panty guy, she thought to herself in horror. The size eleven Brit...

She reeled over how awkward it would be to meet him after the session. Why was this happening to her? At first, she thought she would have to recuse herself at that very moment. But then she determined that she had only met him in passing. It wasn't against the rules. They weren't friends. But was he talking about her? Monique was there in the store that day. Maybe she was the goddess he was mooning over...

This was frustrating and Mona inadvertently spilled Malcolm's coffee on his lap.

"Oh, my! I need to get you a napkin. I'll watch the video again later." She bolted to the restroom and splashed water on her face. "You can handle this, Mona. Just go tell the receptionist. No. No. No. Don't do that. This is going to have to come from inside. A cover-up is in order. This will take the mother of all cover-ups. Command the situation. Stay in control. You can map out your destiny."

Maybe she was overreacting just a tad, but the internship was just too important to her. She could overcome! She would prevail.

She walked back in just in time for the session to be over.

"Gee, Mona. You missed the good stuff. This guy is one sad and lonely man." Malcolm told her. "...uh. You owe me some napkins by the way."

Mona barely heard him. It's time to go shake this man's hand and get it over with. Mona pulled out her reading glasses and hoped that would make her look a little different, but she knew it was no disguise.

As the trio of students filed into the other room, Mona kept looking away, hoping Noel would never see her whole face.

"Excellent. Perfect timing," Mrs. Millhouse said, "These are my interns, Mr. Kensington." She indicated each in turn. "This is Kitty."

Kitty shook Noel's hand like an over caffeinated maniac.

"This is Malcolm."

Malcolm saluted Noel. "Germs..." the male student quipped nervously in a mega tenor croak.

Mrs. Millhouse tried not to laugh. "And this is Mona."

Mona turned around almost completely, pretending to be interested in a psychology book atop Mrs. Millhouse's desk.

Noel started to speak, "Hey! Aren't you...?"

Mona got loud and spoke very, very quickly, "I get that all the time. You were going to say I look like that lady from the cooking shows. Mrs. Millhouse, I decided that Kitty got so much knowledge from taking the last patient aside and having a heart to heart. Can I ask for a few minutes with Mr. Kensington? Oh, I can? You don't mind? Didn't think you would. Great, that's great."

Mona rushed into a corner and waved Noel over to her conspiratorially.

"Uh, that would be fine, as long as he's okay with it." Mrs. Millhouse shrugged to Noel who was looking from the therapist to the would-be shop girl repeatedly as if trying to decide which were the safer choice.

"Oh, I'm sure he's okay right, Mr. Kensington?" Noting his indecision, Mona walked over, grabbed him by the arm, and dragged him away like a helpless lab rat.

"Hi," he said eagerly, like a kid meeting a new puppy at Christmastime.

"Hi," Mona groaned, utterly displeased. She whispered to him. "Look you can't ruin this. This is three months of work. I could lose my scholarship if they find out I didn't recuse myself when I recognized you, a therapy patient. It could be construed as a conflict that we kinda almost met one time, okay, so just go back there and pretend like it never happened."

"Wait a minute," Noel frowned. "This is *so* wrong. You eavesdropped on my darkest secrets, and—you know, don't you—you know I was talking about you?"

"I know," Mona scratched her ear

anxiously, "but honestly I left the room for that part, okay? And, I only heard a little bit. I swear. Anyway, this isn't about you—it's about *me*! Okay, wait. That came out wrong. Let's— oh—let's just—I know—let's go on a date! Just one date. You'd like that right? And you can ask me anything. Anything! As if I were the one in therapy. Turnabout's fair play, right?"

"You're going to go on a date...with me?" Noel blinked. "But...you're doing it for all the wrong reasons. Let's just tell them we have met... Seems simpler to me."

"No!" Mona hollered before she realized she was too loud and began to whisper again. "You don't understand. I can't fail this course. *Please*, just do me this favor. One date. I'll call you tomorrow. Don't say a word." Mona hit Noel in the shoulder a bit too hard. "It'll be fun! You can psychoanalyze me."

"Fine," Noel sighed. "This is all wrong, but I'll keep your secret. To be honest—it would embarrass me more to make a fuss about the whole thing."

"That's the spirit!" Mona smiled.

Kitty looked at Malcolm and crossed her arms over her chest, sticking her nose in the air. "I thought when I did this it was *brown nosing.* Now look at how close she is to him. She is practically sitting in his lap."

"They're standing," Malcolm croaked, causing Kitty to stomp away from him in a huff.

Mrs. Millhouse had slipped into the restroom. When she reentered the room, Noel and Mona walked back toward her, both trying to feign that there was no connection between them what-so-ever.

"Did that help, Mrs. Lawson?" the therapist asked.

"Yes, it was very insightful to talk about what it is really like to be anxious!" Mona replied.

"Great. Mr. Kensington, I will see you again next week without the stardom of all the cameras." She chuckled.

"I can't wait, Mrs. Millhouse," Noel retorted dryly.

Mona stared darts in his direction. He'd keep her secret and she'd make sure of it.

Chapter 11

Mona

Mona tied her hair back in a ponytail and surveyed her heart-shaped face in the bathroom mirror, turning left and then right. She hated it. She didn't look like herself with her hair off her face, but then she was about to do something out of the ordinary, too, so she decided to just go with it.

Dating had never really been a part of her life. She just wanted to get this over with. She had no desire to start a relationship and certainly not with *Noel Kensington*...of all people...

Noel

On the other side of town, Noel was stepping out of a tanning bed. The two weeks he had waited on his big date was a great time to get his body hair waxed and try to look his best. He had been lifting weights in the gym nearly every other day since Mona had set up the date. He was feeling at his peak performance. His eye goggles left a slight whiteness around his eyes, and it was easy to see he had intentionally been going to the tanning bed, but there was no way around that, now was there? The cards are always stacked against poor sods like me, he though. He didn't look *bad*, but there was no hope of winning a woman with his looks alone. He could be honest on that score.

Noel had been reading books about how to be attractive to a woman, what lured them, and kept them interested. He remembered rule number one, "Ask them about *themselves*, and allow them to do most of the talking," he said to his reflection in the gym mirror.

This would be a cinch. He wouldn't even have to pretend. He wanted to know about her. He wanted to know everything about her.

Soon all that was left to do was dress. Noel sprayed three squirts of breath fresh into his mouth and prepared for the drive to her apartment.

She had given him her address. That was a great start. Unless, of course, it turned out to be fake…

Mona

She was not nervous—but she was wearing her mother's perfume for luck.

She had a sinking feeling, though. Noel was like a puppy, she feared. She could be rude, insensitive, unattractive, and unsanitary and he'd probably still follow her around all evening begging for her to bring him home.

That wasn't the worst of it. She was questioning her own choices. How reckless it had been to offer a date to get out of losing a college credit. What was she going to do next, sell her body for crack?

"If only there were some way to get out of this," she said, placing her hands on her hips.

Noel would be there any minute. Mona swallowed, her throat growing tight. She was starting to panic, and her heartbeat grew wild.

In a fit of inspiration, Mona found herself holding a washcloth under the hot water in the kitchen. If she held it to her head and got red and warm, maybe she could tell him she was coming down with something.

No, that wouldn't work. He'd just be kind and ask for a raincheck.

Just as tears sprang to her eyes, a swift knock sounded at the door.

"Coming!" she called.

Finally, Mona opened the door and released a shy smile.

"Oh, my goodness. Are you—is everything

alright? You look—you look like you've been crying, and your forehead is really red." Noel said. "I mean—er—no, no—that's no way to start a date. You look ravishing!" He said it with confidence and flashed his best, brightest smile, showing off all his teeth—and it seemed he'd lived in the States long enough to have decent teeth. "But, um," his smile wavered, "I am a bit worried, are you running a fever?"

"No, no," Mona said awkwardly. "Let's just go do this. Let's have some fun. Just, you do remember I promised *one* date, right. That's all I'm really down for. I'm a very focused student, you know. Don't like a lot of heavy distractions."

Noel shrugged. "That's sad to hear. If you are going on a date with me though—you obviously are giving me some odds, and I have to try." Noel gazed at her like she had the radiance of a star. "I mean look at you. I have written books on the universe and it is just a matter of physics that I should find a new universe with you as my friend."

"Well, I'm glad you put it that way. I'm looking for friends. I'm an only child so I push people away. Go, figure, right?" Mona rolled her eyes. "The *one* I've got is going to run away screaming from me someday. I mean well, but I can also be bossy. So, anyway, let's enjoy our outing, just so long as its crystal clear that I'm not in the market for a relationship. I really like my life the way it is. I—don't judge me—but I was crying—a little—before. The thought of going on a date with any man made me a wreck. There, I did it. I was honest."

"I'm sorry to hear that. I don't like to think of you in tears. But we are discussing way too much in a doorway. Shouldn't we go get something to eat?"

Noel was more charming than Mona anticipated. He was right. It was bumbling for them to have to meet in a doorway and talk about such deep matters, but at least she'd given him the full disclaimer up front. It was a good time to set the parameters, she had calculated, because it was before anything happened. So, what if she was handling her only date in years like it was a hostage negotiation? Desperate times called for desperate measures.

Dinner went well. Better than Mona could have ever dreamed. Noel kept asking about her, no matter how much she dominated the conversation, there he was asking something else. She was running out of details now. She had never been this vulnerable with a man, but Noel had weaseled past her defenses.

Dinner was about finished when Mona excused herself to go to the Ladies' Room, and when she returned, she'd made up her mind about something. "Noel, can we go ahead and get the check? You've been great to me, and I don't deserve it. After all, it's my fault we're here."

"What do you mean?" Noel frowned. "Isn't there one ounce of you that thinks it's fate?"

"If friendships start over fate, then yes. It was fate. But I promise you, no more dating is in the cards for me right now."

"I'm so sorry to hear that." Talk about bad cards. The expression on Noel's face made him look like a guy who had just played a bad poker hand to the river. But when he noticed she was staring; he raised his glass to her. "To friendships, then."

She clinked her glass against his somberly. "Oh please. Don't be so down. I feel terrible for leading you on already. Don't let this make you sad. I will help you find your Mrs. right. That's what friends are for."

"Oh, don't worry about it," Noel said. "You're one of a kind. I probably just need to go and lick my wounds and resign myself to becoming a jolly old, eighty-year-old bachelor."

Mona loved the compliment, but she didn't like anything about the time and place of it. "That is very kind. You are very sweet, and you will not have any trouble finding a woman just like me, but you have got to think about yourself."

Noel signed. "I'm sorry for taking up your time. I feel like a fool."

"Noel! You are not a fool. I'm the fool. Fool is practically my middle name, okay?"

He feigned a little laugh. "I hear you loud and clear, but it isn't making me feel any better. I'm going to pay the check and take you home. It has been one of the best nights of my life. I just need a few days to recover."

"Do exactly that. Take a few days and call me. You should be focusing on therapy right now. Mrs. Millhouse will do everything to get you rebuilt from the ground up. It will only take a few weeks and you'll be out there doing exactly what you love and meeting other fish in the sea. You have nothing to worry about. You are an attractive man, and from what you have told me, I can't help but want to learn more about your research."

"Thanks, Mona."

Noel gave her a ride home and they were both silent as a pair of gravestones the whole way.

At her doorstep, she hugged him and said she had a great time.

And with that Mona had survived the worst. She removed the light smattering of eye make-up and pulled on her sweats, retreating to the couch and knowing she had crushed a man. She stared into the dark room in a catatonic state and began to meditate. Though she did it all the time, she was having difficulty tonight.

Sleep would be the only way to reset after such a miserable experience.

Sleep would help it all to go away.

Chapter 12

Noel

He'd never tell anyone, but during the bleakest and blackest drive home of his life, Noel cried.

He woke up the next morning and he was despondent. It was a hangover that felt as if it contained all the other hangovers in his life, happening all at once. When he could manage, he steadied the bones of his legs and waddled over to the coffee maker.

Noel was in full auto-drive now, reaching for things and turning things on in his kitchen mechanically. He was in a daze until he felt his work clothes sticking to his skin. His dress pants were wet for some unexplainable reason.

For one terrified moment, Noel feared he'd wet the bed. It had been a truly awful night.

But a sloshing sound drew his attention back to the coffee maker. Traitor, Noel thought bitterly, as coffee began to pour straight from the machine into the water catch tray and onto the counter, dripping down and caching on his pants. He had not placed a cup in the machine to catch the brewed java.

In a huff, Noel fumbled for a cup from the cupboard and dropped one on the floor creating new havoc. Glass was everywhere. He tiptoed around the glass shards and went to the door where he had taken off his shoes. He slipped into his freezing cold soaked shoes and saw the muddy footprints on the rug by the door.

"What the hell?" Why would his shoes be wet, too?

There was no time to dwell. Wet, though they were, they'd stop him cutting his toes, so he squished in them back to the dribbling coffee machine. The wet sounds filling the kitchen as he finally stuck a mug under the hot black stream, reminded him there has been rain showers last night.

So, he didn't get to park in the garage... He recalled walking back inside from the car now. There had been walking. There had been crying. There had been rain and lots of bourbon.

On the third Friday of the month, the parking garage was always closed for cleaning so he would have had to park last night two blocks away from his door. He was very angry with himself for driving home, until he started looking for his keys on the rack and the table and his nightstand. They weren't anywhere. He just hoped he had left them in the car and somehow managed to leave it unlocked.

Noel put on some dry clothes and as soon as he walked one block toward his normal parking spot, the sky opened to drop a fresh downpour of rain. It was raining so hard that the whole ground became a series of puddles within a matter of seconds.

Adding defeat to misery, he walked up and down each street becoming one with the hard, cold rain. He couldn't find his car anywhere.

He walked back into his apartment shivering. When he went to the sink to ring out his shirt and grab a kitchen towel for his face, he could see that at that very moment he'd found shelter, the rain outside had stopped.

Noel could do nothing, but sigh and he fetched his cell and called the pub nearest the house. "Ah, it's you," the barkeep answered. "You were in lovely spirits last night Mr. Kensington."

"That's surprising..." Noel shot back. "I recall being a few shots of bourbon away from stepping off a bridge. But more importantly, I'm calling to see if you can help me. I seem to be missing a car." He realized he was on speaker phone when he heard at least three separate voices laughing at his expense.

"Oh. You don't remember the key game?"

"I don't remember anything."

"Well, you seem to take good care of yourself when you drink, let me tell you. After trying to get three people in the bar to take your keys—you devised a way to get rid of them. You grabbed a peanut bowl and suggested a key party. No one was going for it, but we kindly took your keys behind the bar and called you a cab."

"Beautiful," Noel cringed. "I hope I didn't make too much of an ass out of myself. ...I apologize." Laughter sprung out again.

"You weren't making an ass out of anything but your ass," the barkeep chuckled, "a drunk woman kept getting you to flash her 'the moon' as she called it. Mrs. James is a regular and she was celebrating her seventy-fifth birthday. You made her a night she'll always remember."

"Oh, God. I hope you are just having fun at my expense and making all of this up."

"Couldn't make this up if I tried, mate, but you can quit worrying, everyone here loves you."

"That's the problem. I don't usually talk to *everyone* when I drink. I'm pretty much a quiet man."

"It's always the quiet ones." The bar erupted into laughter and cheers and shouts of, "We love you, Noel Roll!"

This day couldn't get any worse. "I've got people calling me Noel Roll. I thought I hated that nickname. Why would I tell anyone about that? Well, I'll be paying Uber Eats to pick up and deliver my car keys. Don't suppose you could make me a bagel or something to pair with the crippling embarrassment?"

"Oh, but we were hoping to see you!"

"I bet..."

"Toasted everything bagel, on the house, mate. Paired with a nice side of car keys. Don't forget to tip your driver."

"Have a nice day." Noel hung up.

#

For weeks Noel avoided his appointments with the therapist, which only intensified his break with all of reality. He had started drinking most nights and he stopped cleaning his apartment. His parents had made many attempts to contact him, but he had become quite adept at putting them off. Ricardo had spent most of his time in Chicago alone since Noel had become quite the solo flyer. It was almost time for Ricardo to go back to his second home in Nebraska, and he pleaded with Noel over the phone, "Please, Noel. Just take a vacation with me to Nebraska for a few weeks. It's got to be this cold windy weather that's destroying you."

"No. There isn't a place to go to escape the hell that is life." Noel was laying on the couch with the phone to his ear in such a way that his apartment appeared to be upside down.

"That's extreme, man. I think you just had a rough couple of months."

"It's just—I can't get her off my mind. If only I had another chance."

"You're not going to get another chance. I think she made that clear. Chick's crazy anyway. Doesn't seem to like other people."

"So, I had one chance and blew it. That's what you're telling me? There's only one of her in the whole world, I had one shot to win her over, and now that's gone."

"Yeah, that's what I'm saying. You need to forget about Mona."

Noel suddenly sat up on the couch, quickly enough to make himself dizzy. "What if I could start all over with her?"

"She's not going to get amnesia, Noel..."

"No..." There was a dead silence for close to thirty seconds.

"No? Noel, are you still there? Look, there's the call waiting. I've got to go, Noel. You're seriously creeping me out. Can't you get back in with the therapist?"

"Forget therapy, man," Noel said, biting his lip. "I think I'm onto something over here. I...I'm going to give myself a second chance."

"Yes, buddy. Give yourself a second chance and move on. There are so many fish in the sea."

"There's only one fish I care about." Noel began to smile, "but the sea is big enough for *more* fish."

"Okay, buddy. Whatever you say. Call me tomorrow and get some rest!" Ricardo hung up the phone.

That was the beginning of Noel's complete break with reality.

Now, his apartment was not only a mess, but it had new additions. In the living room and kitchen were two large chalk boards full of formulas. The bathroom mirror had permanent marker continuing equations from the living room, and there were opened books and physics papers littering the entire place. Most of the books had titles revolving around replication of matter and other frightening topics.

Noel jumped into his car with his disgusting unwashed clothes clinging to his filthy body. His breath smelled of gin and his beard was growing in patches all over his face. He drove to a tiny storage garage he had rented and when opened the door, the sun glinted off the hull of a machine, half-covered in cloth tarp. He pulled away the tarp and dust scattered everywhere.

With a toolbox in tow, he began placing metal pieces within a cabinet in the machine and screwing and fastening parts.

The more he worked, the more determined he became.

#

Nearly three months had passed, and Ricardo had come back to Chicago. He was walking into Noel's apartment carrying a briefcase from his voyage home. He turned a small circle, looking around. "I like it man! You've cleaned up. And, you shaved your beard. I knew you would come to your senses. What made you finally come around?"

"Ricardo! You wouldn't believe it. I've been delving into my work. I have made advances in molecular reproduction that you wouldn't believe."

"That's intense," Ricard said as he took a seat on the couch. "Show me what you've written."

Noel pulled a folder from the coffee table that was full of typed documents, and he let Ricardo browse through it.

"This is amazing work. There are so many formulas in here that I don't understand. In fact, half the material if over my head, but if I'm reading this right, you're theorizing a method for replicating matter with a machine... Wow, the theoretical physics here is astounding. This is really advanced stuff, but I should have known if someone in our circle was going to win the Pulitzer—it would be you."

Ricardo sat back, making himself comfortable and flipping through the file. Then he suddenly sat up. "These schematics... You—you actually built the machine?"

Noel grinned. "I did. I just need to test it. I have a lemon." He tossed the lemon to Ricardo.

Ricard fumbled, but caught it, setting the folder aside. "You're going to attempt to replicate a lemon?"

"Yes. Why not? If it works, we'll know that my machine is finished, and I can move on to larger objects."

"Noel, I—I don't know what to say. This is monumental. I had plans, but they aren't that important. We're going to your machine and I'm going to document this. We're going to go down in history!"

They hurried like excited children outside of Noel's apartment, and as they walked to the car, a homeless man saw the lemon Noel was carrying and said, "I wish that was an apple, I'm hungry."

Noel looked at Ricardo, who only shrugged. "Sorry about that, maybe we'll see you again later."

With that, hey got into the car and drove to the storage space.

Noel uncovered the dusty machine once more.

Ricardo began narrating into his cell phone camera, documenting the event as best he could. After several minutes he navigated to get both his own face and part of the machine in one shot. "Noel Kensington believes that he can systematically reproduce this lemon at an atomic level." Ricardo zoomed onto the lemon panning his cell phone closer to the piece of fruit. "He has placed it into the machine, and he is about to lift the switch and bring another lemon into place beside it."

Ricardo was careful to show how empty the second space was, then zoom out to show both spaces side by side in one view.

"Hit it, brother," he said excitedly.

Noel pulled the switch and a small zap of electricity tingled traveled the length of his body, causing the hair on his head to stand on end. Ricardo must have felt the same thing the camera fell out of Ricardo's hands and onto the floor.

Noel flipped the switch back and the

lights went out in the small storage space, but the machine remained turned on making its loud hum. Ricardo fumbled to pick up the camera and he filmed two lemons which sat under the machine replicator where only one had been before.

"Ok, you can flip the switch, Noel."

Noel frowned at his best friend. "I just did, don't you remember? This is thrilling! How are you not beside yourself right now? We just made history!" Noel was jumping up and down while Ricardo had a puzzled look on his face.

"Noel, how are we going to know if you can actually replicate these two lemons if you don't flip the switch and allow me to catch the miracle on camera?"

"Uh, I don't understand." Noel scratched his head. "Isn't making four lemons from two lemons a bit overboard? After all we just turned one into two. That's simple math. Even a monkey could appreciate what I just did."

Ricardo blinked. "I don't want to argue with you, but you brought these two lemons here to see if we could replicate them, and now you're getting cold feet. It's not like you."

"Ricardo! *Ricardo*? You're not kidding at

all..." Noel found himself pressing the back of his hand to his mate's forehead to feel if he might be feverish. "It's like you have dementia."

Ricardo drew up, insulted. "What is that supposed to mean!?"

Noel sighed. "You're going to have to trust me. We came here with one lemon. There was only ever one, I swear."

"Now that's not possible. Noel, I've been at your side since we left your place. I've got it all on video. Just watch the footage."

For a second Noel was certain Ricardo was playing some elaborate trick on him, but they rewound the video, and Noel was amazed to see an entire reality take place in the cell video different from the one he lived. It was parallel. It had the same people in it and similar events. The time stamp matched accurately, but he knew for a fact that the events Ricardo had lived and recorded did not match the reality Noel had just witnessed.

Noel swallowed. "Ricardo. You must believe me, you must! There's some sort of unforeseen side-effect at play. I was the one who flipped the switch, so for some reason I am the only one who remembers what really happened... Oh my God, instead of physically replicating the matter, alone, the machine has altered the timeline, created an entire thread of time and space where the replicated matter can exist! I don't know how to explain it any other way, and I'm sure faulty wiring was the cause, but in one way it worked, but in another it's completely scary..."

Ricardo watched Noel skeptically as if he, too, were trying to work out if his friend and colleague were playing a joke on him. The he scratched his head and swallowed hard. "I'm going to give you the benefit of the doubt that what you're saying is true... You set out to replicate one lemon and it worked. For you, it worked. As for me, I'm trapped in a parallel timeline where there always were two lemons... Interesting. You're right... Noel, this is completely scary."

Noel bit his lip. "Wait a minute. What else changed? What if things outside of you and me and this bloody lemon were also altered?"

Ricardo's eyes went wide. "Man, I don't know. I can't even really help on that score. You're the only one with any perception of an altered history."

Noel held his head in his hands. "This is bad..."

"Wait a minute! Let's approach this logically. I, for one, remember a homeless man outside of your place. Did your reality include a homeless man?"

"Yes!" Noel exclaimed.

"Excellent, so my homeless fellow definitely saw two lemons—he even said, 'one more and you can make lemonade.' Let's ask him and let him clear it up."

"No, no, no!" Noel shouted. "That's not what happened in my timeline. Are you sure he didn't say he wished the lemon were an apple?"

"No. Why would he say that?"

"He was hungry, and we were walking around the neighborhood with a lemon! My God, this is frightening. I've got to see is anything else has changed!" Noel covered the machine and shut off the lights.

They drove home silent about the whole situation.

Chapter 13

Noel

Noel spent weeks reading the news and researching history books—reading topics on the internet. His search bar was full of queries like, "When did the Titanic sink?" and "notable eighteenth century European authors." He couldn't research every topic known to man, but he had tried to ascertain if anything crucial was different in this new world which he had inadvertently made.

After determining that nothing significant had changed—Hitler was still dead, most of humanity accepted that the world was round—he felt much calmer and was finally able to take a comfortable nap, without the fate of mankind weighing down upon his shoulders.

He laid across the couch, his eyelids growing heavy, contemplating what had happened.

What a beautiful, shocking, unexpected avenue the universe had taken to alter matter... If his theory was correct, his machine could copy cells and atoms, but the powers that be didn't leave things there. The universe bent around this copied matter, and it created a new world, a path of "least possible resistance" to a time and place where that copy could exist. Or as he liked to put it, "The world makes a place for a replicated object by creating its own unique, elegantly simple history."

Noel wanted a second lemon. But the moment his machine created it, the universe rewrote a history in which that lemon sprung from a seed, grew from a tree, was carefully plucked, purchased by Noel on a grocery trip he remembered only supplying him with a single lemon, not two, and ultimately allowed two perfect yellow fruit to be drooled over by a hungry and thirsty homeless man.

When Noel fell asleep, he had a dream that he was in a serene and wonderful, loving relationship with Mona. They lived together. They ate together. They watched TV together, attended lectures. She even taught him Krav Maga.

When Noel woke, he had the sinking feeling of reality snapping back into place. He lived alone. He watched TV alone. He didn't know the first thing about Krav Maga. He was still so incredibly single.

Noel sighed and tried counting his blessings, but it was difficult. The bar where he had lost his keys had begun to accept him as a regular. He was quickly becoming a black out drunk, night after night, trying to drown the pain and loneliness and depression. He was very fortunate that he had royalties coming in from his published articles or he would have lost all semblance of a normal life.

He knew he should try to break the cycle, but he felt powerless. He chased the bottle hard, even threw some shots into the routine. Why not? But his mind went to a darker place than it ever had before...

The idea was as terrible as it was brilliant, and Noel knew he couldn't outrun it.

He would do it because in many ways his entire life was leading to this point.

He took a taxi home to his apartment grabbing a six pack of beer and retrieving the hairbrush Mona had left in his car from his closet where he had hidden it like a treasure. It wasn't just a small piece of her, it was a memento he could pretend he intended to return. It would give him an opening to see her again. But now it was so much more. It was his salvation.

He pulled a strand of red hair from it and walked to his car. He felt suddenly more sober than ever before. Make history? Win the Pulitzer? Noel wanted none of those things.

What he wanted was Mona. Why make history, when he could literally make her?

There was no thinking about it. There was no waiting to change his mind or weigh the consequences. Noel sped quickly to his storage space and typed away at the computer for hours. He placed the hair inside the machine's compartment, and he pulled the switch.

Noel's fingers tingled and twitched as the electricity passed through his body. Every nerve ending sang and he realized the truth...

Mona was probably the only reason he had built the machine in the first place.

#

Noel woke up with a complete sense that he had done something terrible, but he couldn't remember exactly what it was. His head was sending off all kinds of bells and alarms to tell him he had overdone it once again. He looked up at the ceiling and noticed he wasn't in his bed. He should have known because the moment he tried to move; a searing pain shot up his rigid spine. It took some effort, but he pushed himself up from the cold concrete of the storage space and held his hand on his hips with his back stiff and throbbing.

After letting out a wince of discomfort he managed to climb to his feet and make small steps over to the roll-up door which he shook to prove he had not even tried to lock it before passing out. He went over in his head how he could be stupid enough to sleep in a storage space. And, he couldn't help but think his deposit would never get returned. Yet, in the back of his mind he knew there was something far worse he had done. But what was it?

He looked over his opened laptop to see that he had programmed for hours to find a way to replicate a human person from a small piece of DNA. He arched a brow. His machine had all kinds of makeshift additions on it, and he reasoned that there must have been no way he succeeded. It shouldn't be possible... Carefully, he began to look around the storage unit. There was no woman here—it must have failed. Brushing it off with a huge sigh of relief, Noel went out to his car and checked his cell phone messages.

The moment the phone screen came to life, however, he noticed an incredible anomaly. He had missed calls. Several missed calls. They weren't from Mum or Da or Ricardo or his sister or work or even from his niece or the bar that he frequented almost every night. No, the calls were from Mona.

That wasn't right. Why would the object of his unrequited love be calling?

On a hunch he checked the call history and gasped to find last night was just the tip of the iceberg. They called each other daily. There weren't just missed calls in his call log, they'd talked for hours.

This could not be real. There were even saved voice mail messages from Mona. He scrolled through and chose what seemed to be the oldest one.

"Noel," said Mona's sweet voice, "I know we haven't talked since the date, but my twin sister is in town and I want to make a good impression on her fiancé. Yet, again—I must stress this isn't a date, but she has been treating me terribly since I was a child about never having a boyfriend. She doesn't understand it and won't leave me alone about it. I figured we could start that friendship we were talking about with a little masquerade."

"What? A masquerade?" Noel said aloud, both panicked and intrigued by this new turn of events. Noel thought he was dreaming, so he pinched himself and when that didn't work, he shook his whole body like a dog and tried to blink his way to the waking world. It wasn't a good dream because it was as if all his fears had been compounded into a singular terror. He was almost certain that at some point during their date Mona had mentioned being an only child.

If he had done this—if he had tried to replicate her and succeeded, he would have to put mad scientist at the top of all his future resumes. He'd been too drunk to realize the ramifications of history altering and rewriting to accommodate an entirely new human being. How much had having one more Lawson girl affected the world at large? It was the lemon all over again. A change this big could have terrible consequences. War, famine, stock market crashes, extinction level events...

"What the hell have you done, Noel? YOU BLOOMING IDIOT! YOU HAD TO BE BLOODY STUPID AND DRINK YOURSELF INSANE!!!"

It looked like he would have to spend a whole day researching the internet again to see what he had changed in the world. Luckily, he had good practice with this sort of thing. Gravity, the planets, the end of the Cold War... Things seemed very much the same as far as the history of mankind.

Noel has even noticed getting out of the car that the same lost kitten sign hung on the nearby lamp post at the end of his street. "You played God all because of some Guinness, Noel! Changed the world and created another Mona! You don't even know which one is the new one! And, that alone is proof you shouldn't have done it..."

He plopped down on the couch, his head beginning to pound. In a perfect world he would be sharing all his findings with his peers in the field of science, but how could he tell other academics what he had done? He knew that no one would believe him, and that the practical introduction of the new material was akin to the invention of the atom bomb. Noel didn't want to be another Oppenheimer.

"Ricardo! You've got to come over!" He screamed into the cell phone receiver in desperation.

"Are you daft, Noel? I am in Nebraska. I told you to get help before I left."

"I did it, Ricardo. I got drunk and I—I made another Mona."

"What, you've got to be kidding me. There are so many medications you should be on right now."

"I couldn't help myself. I was drunk and I had found a way to duplicate her with DNA. It was genius really; something I never could have come up with sober. I pulled out all the stops."

"This is completely insane. Well, is she there with you? Is she healthy, is she mentally aware?"

"Uh, no, she's not here now. Remember what happened last time?"

Ricardo cursed. "You mean do I remember reality altering to fit the second lemon. Yes, Noel, I'll never forget it to my dying days... So, reality changed again? What's different this time?"

"Uh, so, near as I can tell, in my reality she and I never spoke again. But in this new reality Mona has a twin sister and her twin sister is engaged and she like wanted to go on a double date so she called me up."

"I thought she hated dating," Ricardo groaned.

"She called it a masquerade," Noel explained. "I think she just wanted to seem like she was in a normal relationship for once so her sister wouldn't give her grief."

"Well, I hate to break it to you, buddy, but you told me Mona was a twin weeks ago."

"No, no," Noel complained. "That can't be right. I'm positive she was an only child before I tried to clone her!"

"Calm down, Noel." Ricardo sighed heavily. "I'm no good to you right now. The new reality, the one that's new to you, I live in it, remember? I don't remember your reality, just like I only ever knew two lemons whereas you remember when there was only one... Look, the damage is done. There's no changing it. Even if you thought of a way to reverse this catastrophe, I'm convinced you'd only make it worse. When is this double date? Do you think you went on it already or is it like still coming up soon?"

"Hold on a second." Noel checked his phone. According to his calendar the double date was next week! "You're never going to believe this, Ricardo, the double date with her twin is next week. It hasn't happened yet."

Ricardo laughed. "Good. I want you to go. I want you to make the most out of this opportunity, man. But listen to me, Noel. You have to swear to destroy the machine. I don't care how big a genius you are; you are lucky things didn't turn out far worse. I'm just sorry I didn't get to see things happen the way you did. But listen, Noel, you deserve this second chance. You helped me when I hit rock bottom. Just promise me you won't alter matter or history ever again."

Noel ran weary fingers through his hair. "I promise."

Noel felt so much better after hanging up the phone. He had found some way to mix his complete melt down with some small picture of getting his life back on track. It wasn't just that he was going to get to see Mona again. Now he knew how dark and insane his life could get if he let it. He could not—would not allow that to happen again.

Over the course of the next few days, Noel cleaned up his life in every way a life could be cleaned. He stopped drinking, he cleaned his apartment, he went to the gym regularly, even improved his diet. For the first time in ages he felt motivated to turn a near complete one-eighty.

The only thing Noel hadn't accomplished yet was destroying the machine. He didn't want to see it. He didn't want to revisit that dark, drunk hour when he had done the unthinkable. So, he put it off. The longer he avoided the storage unit, the more it felt like he had never plucked that hair from that hairbrush and all things were as they were meant to be.

It felt as if it were all a bad dream, a delusion he'd never revisit again.

All that was left to do was enjoy a second date with the woman who had never even wanted to go on the first one.

Chapter 14

Noel

Noel had a gentle splash of cologne on his neck and a song in his heart as he pulled the car into park and dialed Mona's cell to let her know he had arrived to pick her up.

She wasn't picking up the call and Noel jumped a little when the passenger door opened, and Mona slipped right in. "How have you been, Noel? You look nice. Oh, you smell nice, too. I hope you aren't trying to impress me. I promise this is just for show."

Same old Mona. That much hadn't changed. He sniffed. "I just wanted to make a good impression. Tell me again why we're pretending like we are dating?"

"It's just to get my sister off my back, okay?" She buckled herself in.

Noel pulled back out into traffic. "Okay, well, this is your show, why don't you explain the details."

"Cool, so I have it all planned out," Mona explained while Noel drove. "We have been dating for a year. We met when you were visiting campus to give a lecture. You don't have to lie about your work. Just tell her about physics and stuff. What topic do you know the most about?"

Noel's palms began to sweat. "Let's just say I'm pretty good with replication of matter."

"Oh wow. Theoretical physics is amazing. Won't it be insane the day they actually crack it?"

"Oh yeah. Insane. Maybe someday they'll get there..." He chuckled nervously.

"Well that's pretty interesting, just tell her you were lecturing about that, and that I ran into you and knocked the folder out of your hands and we just bumped heads trying to pick up the papers. Then, you asked me out on a date." Mona smiled. She had a radiant smile.

Noel tried to focus on the road. "So, the typical Professor meets student love affair. How great would it have been if we really had met that way?"

"You wish," Mona rolled her eyes. "That's every man's fantasy."

"You know," Noel said calmly, "there's a lot about me you don't know. I'm actually happy we met the way we did. I just don't think you understand how special—anyway—never mind... This is no time for chit chat. So, I know you study Psychology. What don't I know about you that I would know after a year of getting to know you better? Let's see… Do you have many friends? That might come up, right?"

"My best friend is Monique."

"Oh, that's cute—such a close name. Mona and Monique…"

"I know we love it," Mona grinned. "Actually, you've met her. You saw us together at Versace. She has a dog named Heather Dog and she lives on the third floor down the road from me. She is very neurotic, and super funny. She's got the comedic timing of a stand-up comic."

Noel nodded. "So, neurotic gal pals are alright, you just don't like neurotic men, like me?" His brows lifted helplessly.

"Oh, Noel, don't say that about yourself," Mona said, patting his shoulder. "You're not like that at all."

Noel huffed. "Oh, I think you would be surprised."

"Well anything else—we just make it up as we go, okay? If I correct you just go with it, and if we start on a tangent, let's continue down it together. It'll be fun!"

Mona seemed almost eager for this charade. Her energy was very upbeat. "I like that," Noel replied. "Pure improv... I didn't think this masquerade was going to be fun, but I enjoy spending time with you, Mona. I hope you know that."

"Friendship isn't all that bad after all. We'll have to hit up a bookstore some time, find you a smart girl, woman of your dreams. She's out there, Noel. You've just got to learn to relax."

Noel softly sighed. "Well, I'm sure I could settle for second place." He thought that might be an endearing thing for a woman to hear, but Mona was looking out the window at the lights of the city. She hadn't even heard him. He might as well be talking to himself.

As Noel pulled up to the valet Mona was readily stepping out onto the curb to hug her sister who was waiting. Noel got out second and walked over to her and almost gasped at the similarities. There was the same heart-shaped face, the same auburn hair. Mona's sister was more like her than any natural twin could be. Of course, he knew in the back of his mind that they weren't natural twins, they were literally the same matter duplicated—duplicated by him, in fact, his science.

"Noel, this is my sister Rachael and her fiancé Spencer," Mona said.

Rachael was as magnificent as Mona was, but Spencer wasn't much to look at. He was overly tall, lankly, and a bit pale. He was also the luckiest bastard in the universe. Who knows who Spencer would be dating if Noel hadn't split the proverbial atom at the behest of a pack of beers? Certainly, it wouldn't have been Mona's perfect twin. It wasn't fair. If Mona knew half of what Noel was capable of, she'd be dreaming about him the same way he dreamt of her.

When he came back down to earth, Noel realized his mission here was to be the knight in shining armor. There was only one Noel, so he had to be the best Noel he could possibly be.

"Nice to meet you both," Noel said with a soft smile.

Rachael drove her elbow into Mona's ribs, "He's quite the looker, Mona. I can see why you were hiding him from me for so long."

Spencer frowned and Rachael squeezed his shoulder. "Don't be jealous, honey, you're a looker, too, babe." Rachael winked at her fiancé.

Noel wished Mona felt the way her sister

did. "I appreciate you saying that, but I assure you it's purely platonic between us." He didn't know why he said it. It had just come out. He could feel his face begin to redden. He'd ruin the whole masquerade before it even really began! His chest burned and he wondered if he was doing it out of spite.

Mona laughed very loudly with the worst heckle giving Noel the death stare. "Oh, he is so modest. And funny! Platonic? Yeah right, lover, if dating for a whole year is just platonic. I hope you don't feel that way about me after dating me for sooooo long, honey?" She said to Noel, squeezing his forearm.

He swallowed. "Oh, I was just kidding, *darling*." Noel gave her the impression he wasn't through with his ribbing, but that he would play along.

"Well," said Spencer drily, "It's chilly out here. We should get inside."

No one laughed or smiled. Spencer did not have the comedic timing Mona had attributed to her friend Monique. That was for sure.

None-the-less, they filed into the restaurant.

"So, Rachael. It's almost like you came out of nowhere. Where have you been?" Noel found himself being completely passive aggressive with the whole situation. He was frustrated on levels that he had never even imagined before. He was irritated that Mona was using him, that the world was different, that he had no chance of getting the love he so desperately wanted, and that all his new findings would have to remain a secret. What he didn't realize, in the moment, was that he was more frustrated with himself—that he couldn't get Mona, and that he had lost his mind for the last three months and done inconceivable things.

"Oh, didn't Mona tell you? I have been studying to finish my degree in Ireland. You sound like you have a little bit of an Irish accent yourself, by the way..."

Noel smiled. "I thought it was barely noticeable. I grew up in the United Kingdom, but my parents moved to the States when I was still a boy."

"I should have known with a name like Noel." Rachael turned and ordered her food, and Mona asked for the same thing.

Noel spit his water back into his cup when they ordered the same way, down to the condiments and sides. "Are you both getting the same meal?" Noel had turned to the scientist within and began observation. If nothing else, he could see what the fruits of his experiment were.

"It happens all the time," Rachael explained with a wave of her hand. "It's my fault. I have great taste." She laughed. "I'm only kidding, Noel. It's a twin thing. Even when we're apart we sometimes find ourselves watching the same movie or buying the same things at the store. It's eerie." Rachael smiled.

"I'm sure your shared connection is even more uncanny than the typical twin experience." Noel could barely hold back his secret. He wanted to blurt out that he had done all of this himself, but it wasn't ever going to happen. He knew the earth wasn't ready for his genius and that these people would call him a lunatic. Talking to Rachael was getting frightening. He didn't even want to know what he would learn next. Noel turned to Spencer. "Spencer, you haven't told us much about yourself, mate."

Mona was quiet, but she was making lots of eye contact and laughed at things Noel had said. In fact, her eyes were pleasantly on Noel for most of the night, but he decided it had to be part of her act.

"I'm just Spencer," he said quietly. "I like steak and potatoes, and she and I met in Gloucestershire. I really do like Chicago, but as soon as we got outside the airport, Rachael almost blew away with the wind."

Noel chuckled. Spencer was a bit of a dork, but he had a funny side, too. "Tell us more about how you met."

Spencer started to say a little more, and just at that moment Mona and Rachael both sneezed, coughed, and apologized in unison.

"Oh my God, it's scary when you do that!" Spencer looked shaken up, and Noel just sat amazed at the fruit of his labor.

"What the hell was that?" Noel had to pry.

"Oh, we've been doing—," Mona started.

"That since we were—," Rachael finished.

"Kids." They both said the last word together. Then Spencer, Mona, and Rachael chuckled together.

"Spencer thinks it's cute." Rachael kidded.

Noel sat with his mouth open. He again worried that he had done something terribly, terribly wrong, against man and against science.

"What really scares people isn't that we finish each other's sentences, or get sick at the same time, but that we have written the same short stories! They tested us when we were children and we wrote the same narrative word for word in different rooms." Mona explained.

Noel's throat constricted with anxiety. "Oh, that *is* uncanny."

"I guess you don't remember me telling you all about that on our dates, Noel. Silly Noel, if he only listened better." Mona chided.

Noel didn't know if she was serious or lying. He was having trouble differentiating between realities.

"You look shaken up, Noel. Are you okay?" Rachael asked.

"Yes, I think I need to be excused." Noel took four steps toward the men's room, paused to grab his aching head, and then walked the rest of the way very hastily. He splashed cold water on his face and reassessed himself in the mirror. An elderly man walked in and noticed him at the sink trying to get a grip.

"Hey, young man. Don't be nervous. I saw you with those twin knockouts." The old man winked. "What is it they say? Best put a ring on that one, sonny. You can do it! She's into you. Was hanging on every word you said. You can get her. Heck, its amazing to see two such good looking gals in one place! Don't let her slip away now."

"Yeah, two in one place. I-imagine that." Noel stammered.

The old man continued his pep talk, "God don't make no mistakes, now does he, sonny! The two of you must be together tonight for a reason! Go back out there and tell her how you feel! Women love that."

"Oh. Yes. God. God doesn't make mistakes, but I make some pretty big ones." Noel sighed.

The old man grimaced. "I don't know what you done, boy, but you got to forgive yourself first. You got to get over yourself and go back out there and win the lady before it's too late!"

Noel wondered why he was having such a lengthy conversation in a bathroom, but elderly people had always been strange to him. He decided that he had to reprioritize what he truly thought was strange anyway. Noel was highly considering putting himself at the top of the chain as the strangest thing he could fathom. Noel chose to finish the pep talk in the mirror, "Ok, boy. You can do this. Just go with it. Like the old man said, go win the girl!"

He sat down at the table and began to chew on his food and there was silence at the table, almost a return to relative normalcy, when, out of the blue, Mona and Rachael both started singing *We've Only Just Begun* by the Carpenters. He swallowed hard and looked at Spencer, who was nodding his head and humming along as if it were something the twins did all the time.

"...life ahead/ We'll find a place where there's room to grow/ And yes, we've just begun..." the twin beauties sang. This couldn't be normal. Noel began choking and the girls stopped singing to both hit him on the back, which only made him choke the more.

"Man, your boyfriend is suddenly a nervous wreck." Rachael noted to Mona.

"I know, we don't double date much." Mona responded. "Noel, honey, are you going to be alright?"

Noel nodded and managed to swallow his food.

"Well, enough about Spencer and I, Mona, how did you two meet?" Rachael asked.

"I'll take this one, darling." Noel looked at Mona and started his masterpiece. "I was giving a lecture at her college and I was walking to my car completely bothered about a thesis I had to write when out of nowhere screams this fire truck, sirens blaring, going full-speed in the opposite direction, drawing my attention. I didn't even see Mona coming, but she slammed into me full on, sending my papers flying into a frenzy—"

"Just like a movie." Spencer had a mouthful of food, but had to chime in.

"I know, cliché isn't it?" Noel couldn't stop because he was on a roll. "We picked up the papers and I noticed her face for the first time. It totally caught me by surprise. I saw the most attractive woman I had ever seen in my life." Noel reached over and curled a strange of auburn hair behind Mona's ear. "I asked her to coffee and the rest is history."

"Oh, that is so cute!" Rachael smiled and hugged Mona. "I'm so glad you have a boyfriend; I was going to have an intervention if you didn't. You always think about your ambitions, Mona. It is healthy to make time for others in the quest for self-improvement, but why am I telling you this—you seem to have finally caught on."

Mona was quiet, her eyes contemplative. She seemed pleased with Noel's acting prowess.

"Well dinner was amazing!" Spencer chirped. "You Yanks know your steak!"

The waiter came by and asked if anyone had room for dessert. Noel had always gotten dessert by himself, but he felt the table was through with the meal, and he wanted badly to get away from this sham of a date. He loved spending time with Mona, but he would have given anything for it to be under different circumstances. To prolong it was only going to hurt worse.

The four of them each said goodnights and formalities as the valet brought Noel his car. He opened the door for Mona and decided to take his beating on the car ride home. Any perfect love story would end up with her being completely fascinated with him and coming up to his room to end the night, but now with Mona. She was still one tough cookie. She'd probably have a list of the things he'd done wrong instead.

As soon as they drove away, Mona started in, "Again, Noel. Thank you. You are such a good friend."

He could have had a coronary right then and there. "There you go with the friend thing again, Mona. I told you, you don't have to keep reminding me we're not going to get together. I have multiple degrees in science. I understand. If there is one thing in the world I can't have—it is a relationship with Mona Lawson." His agitation was starting to grow. What hadn't he done for this woman?

"That's great! You get it... Monique and I are going to watch the new Bruce Willis movie tomorrow. Do you know the one?"

Noel didn't understand why she was changing the subject. "I know the one you mean. The sequel. You know, its going to be exactly like the previous four."

"I know. Monique wants to see it because she thinks he is sexy." Mona arched a brow. "But I have seen too many action movies that fit the same mold. What I have yet to see is a good romance. It's been years."

"The most underrated romance in history has got to be *Charade*," Noel put in. "People really did a good job of spoofing more serious matters back then, and it has just enough hilarity to seem like an actual relationship."

Mona practically jumped out of her seat. "That's classic, Noel! You watch old movies! You call *Charade* a romance! I thought I was the only one who did that. She was perfect in *Breakfast at Tiffany's*. That's a true romance!"

Noel smiled. He would never have guessed he and Mona had this in common. "Yeah. People don't make movies the way they used to. You know, they're playing the movie in its entirety at the theater downtown next weekend. Would you like to go?"

The moment the question left his lips he realized the sin he'd just committed. But he hadn't even been thinking, it just came out and there was no sense backtracking now.

"Well..." Mona paused.

It felt like the longest pause in the history of mankind. Planets turned. Tides went out and came back in again. Entire civilizations were born, met their heights of human achievement, then disappeared like ghosts.

At last Noel couldn't await her answer a second longer. "I'm sorry," he started. "No, what am I saying?" He laughed. "I'm not sorry. It was an honest question, okay? It just came out. It felt natural, that's all, and I can feel you calming up with tension now because you're afraid I'll think we are going on a real date."

"Wait, Noel, no. I wasn't going to say that," Mona whispered.

"Well you thought it. It's alright—I'm giving a lecture in Nebraska next week anyway. Almost completely forgot."

Mona was quieter than usual. "That sounds interesting. What's it about?"

"It's about some nerve-racking material replication theories."

"Ah, ha. More theoretical physics. Do you think you'll ever really be able to duplicate something?"

"You'd be surprised."

"Noel, I'm genuinely interested here. I love science. Why do you sound so secretive suddenly? Is it top secret? Quiet everyone, Noel works for the CIA!" She laughed.

Noel licked his lips. "Well, we're getting close to your apartment. I just wanted to tell you something before you go." He felt a rush of energy. He was going to spill his guts and tell

her that she meant everything to him. He
wanted to tell her that he would drop the world
to make her happy. But he just gasped for air
and said. "Oh, it's nothing." That old guy from
bathroom would be very disappointed.

Mona's eyes lashes fluttered. "Well, if you
think of it, give me a call. Maybe we can get
coffee next week. Call me when you're back
from your trip. Thanks for doing me a solid
today, buddy. I mean it." She hit him on the
shoulder like she was his baseball coach and
he'd played a good game, before she jumped out
to whistle her way toward her apartment.

Noel just sat and watched as his world
caved in on him once again.

Chapter 15

Noel

The word "buddy" played over and over in his head the entire drive home.

He sat at his dining room table staring at a bottle of gin. When he turned it in his hands, the liquid caught the moonlight. "You can have one shot to take the edge off, Noel, but you know what happened the last time..."

Noel hesitated, then poured and drank one shot and just kept saying "buddy" over and over, out loud, until he threw his tie into the trash can and fell asleep on the couch curled up in a ball.

#

Two days later Noel found himself stepping off the airplane and walking into the Lincoln airport. As soon as he walked into his arrival gate, he saw Ricardo standing there with a sign that said "John Travolta." It made him laugh and it was the most genuinely belly laugh he'd had in days.

"Nobody actually thought you were picking up John Travolta. What would he be doing in Lincoln?" Noel hugged Ricardo.

"You'd be surprised. One lady stood here with me for a half hour before her plane got called. It was just the right amount of stupid that someone would fall for it." Ricardo winked.

"Gullible Hillbillies," Noel smirked.

"Hey, don't hate on American Hill People, Noel. They've got guns. Anyway, how are you? I hope you have gotten all the crazy out of your system?"

Noel frowned. "What do you mean?"

"If you don't remember—I thought you were going to get locked up with all that creating something from nothing nonsense."

"Oh, that. Well, let's just say I learned my lesson about all of that."

Ricardo opened the passenger door for Noel to climb into his car. "I don't know how you could ever learn your lesson. Have you gotten over her, yet?"

Noel filled his lungs with air. "I will never get over her. We went on the date and she hasn't called me since. I...I did leave her a couple of messages."

Ricardo rolled his eyes. "Big mistake. You shouldn't come off as desperate, Desperado. I've got just the thing for you. We're going to the strip club."

"Oh, God, Ricardo, no. I told you we were never doing that again. I don't think I could ever. That place was sleazy."

"Look, Noel, forget about the cleanliness of the place. I know a stripper and she is going to come home with you so long as you don't freak her out with any of that nonsense about creating something from nothing. She's not big into science, okay?"

"Ricardo," Noel groaned. "I need to get a shower just from imagining this girl and whatever place you were planning on taking me. Is there a clinic where I can stop and get tested? I think you gave me a host of STD's with just the idea itself..." Noel stuck out his tongue.

"Your loss, man. She's a ten, buddy. And she'll get your mind off Melissa or whatever her name is."

"Mona. I think you knew that." Noel scowled.

Ricardo threw up his hands in defeat. "Let's go. You have a lecture to give in two hours."

Noel smiled. "About that. I'm going to

rehearse it with you in the car.”

“I wouldn’t expect anything less...”

They drove to Ricardo’s house, which was only a few miles from the college. Noel showered there and shaved and was ready to deliver the speech of a lifetime.

After hours of hitting every topic he had rehearsed the speech was a success. Students were asking questions for a half hour after the lecture which meant not only had they listened, but they wanted to know more.

After the speech he went into the Dean’s office and met with a lady who paid him a generous check for making the appearance. It was enough to cover his exploits for months. He smiled about living his old life without constantly thinking about Mona. It was refreshing to think about what he could do on his own, especially when he didn’t give in to depression and alcohol.

He could have continued his streak of self-discovery had it not been for Ricardo and his off-putting desires to get Noel on the path to true raucous bachelorhood. They stood over the kitchen counter back at Ricardo’s house. “Okay, you look good Noel. Keep the suit. We’re going out. I’m buying the drinks and we’re taking a

Lyft.”

Noel scratched his chin. It was a nice suit and Ricardo never wore it. “I don’t know, Ricardo. Last time I drank I used the stupid machine.”

“Machine. Machine. You didn’t flip any switch on any stupid machine. The more I think about, the more I think the whole thing was a drunken delusion. And, if you did—it didn’t do anything. You saw extra lemons, I didn’t. Stop kicking your own ass, Noel. Life does a good enough job of kicking our asses for us. Tonight, is a night to let it go.” Ricardo leaned in conspiratorially. “Cotton Candy Andi is her name.”

Noel tried not to gag. “She sounds too sweet for me. I have sensitive teeth, and an even more sensitive libido.”

Ricardo patted Noel on the back. “Drink a few drinks and I know you become whatever you always wanted to be. Here, here. Do a shot of whiskey with me.”

Ricardo poured two shots of whiskey and screamed, “*Salud!*” as they knocked them back. Pretty soon, Noel got a rush of alcohol-fueled adrenaline.

#

"And, then she called me 'buddy'! The nerve, I mean, after I bought dinner, and we laughed about old movies. Who knows how much more we have in common?" The stripper was putting her naked butt right in his face. She got on his lap and shook her breasts at him. "She has a twin sister. I really can't see anything going right without her. I made her sister in a lab."

"That's it!" Cotton Candy Andi groaned. She got up out of Noel's lap and left him sitting in his chair to slouch over as if he had fallen asleep where he sat. He was so drunk he kept talking even after she left.

Andi waltzed over to Ricardo, "Here's your thousand dollars back—your pal is worthless. He keeps going on about his wife."

"What, no! That's not even his wife. It's just a woman he wants to date. Besides, no one can resist you, Andi! Go back over there and make him forget his own name," Ricardo instructed.

Andi shook her head. "That's even more pathetic. He doesn't even know what he's saying. Said he made her sister in a lab? You're not paying me enough to listen to that all night.

Sorry, Ricky, I'm done."

Ricardo sighed and slipped his friend a few bills. "Here is two hundred for putting up with him this long. You're still my favorite, Andi." He grabbed Noel by the arm and pulled him up from where he sat. "Come on buddy, the Lyft is outside waiting."

Noel was still talking. "...Doesn't want to go see *Breakfast at Tiffany's* with me...? Buddy...buddy...*buddy*." Noel was mumbling and didn't care who was listening.

#

The next morning Noel woke up to the smell of coffee and breakfast. Ricardo had called out for delivery. He wasn't the type to cook for his friends when they were in town, but he had sat the food out like a buffet. Noel drank a few sips of coffee holding his head. "I can't drink. I swear I can't drink without getting a bloody hangover!"

"This is exactly what you need—some biscuits and eggs! That will have you feeling—"

Noel ran to the bathroom and began heaving a night of drinking into the toilet.

When Noel emerged back into the dining area, his teeth were minty fresh.

"Did you say biscuits? Sounds good to me." Noel ate enough breakfast to replace all the nutrients he had lost. He took a shower and started feeling better around noon.

He and Ricardo spent the next few days binging the latest zombie series and shopping for Noel's parents, but the whole time Noel kept lightly breaching the topic of his unrequited love. He tried not to do it, but every time he did, Ricardo left the room like a babysitter at the end of his rope.

Finally, it was time to say good-bye again. At the airport, Ricardo put his arm around his best friend. "I can't stand to see you this way anymore. I'm being serious now. Nothing I've tried to do for you has worked. You need to get help, Noel. The same way you encouraged me to get help with my gambling. I hope it works out for you, bud, I really do."

Noel got on the plane and sat next to an attractive woman with flowing blonde hair. It wasn't long before she told him she was a swimsuit model. Any man would have died to get a moment with her since she was throwing out all the signs of being single in his direction, but he occupied the hours of the flight telling her about Mona.

Eventually, she must have tired of

hearing the name of a woman repeatedly—a woman that was not her. She popped in some ear buds and leaned over for a nap. After he drove the swimsuit model away, Noel was stuck with his own thoughts for hours.

The worst of his defeatist thoughts was this one: There were two of them. He had broken space and time to make two Monas and neither of them wanted to love him.

His maddening thoughts lead him to contemplate cloning her again, but he very quickly rejected the thought in his mind. It was as if he had an angel and a devil on his shoulders.

The devil was bright red and wore a mustache and a forked tail. "But, just one more Mona would have to solidify things. Look at how much closer you got with just making one more Mona! Got you a second date, didn't it?"

The angel had a long beard and resembled the old man from the bathroom. He has powdery white wings and a crooked golden halo. "You're a better man of science than to go meddling in these forces again, Noel, especially for selfish gain. Where's your conscience? You can't go on making clones of people to get what you want out of life. Can you imagine what this world or your chaotic life would be like if you solved every problem by cloning people?"

Noel suddenly shook himself. He was alone on a plane seated next to a beautiful woman who had actually wanted to pass the time talking with him and instead he was imagining demons and angels and contemplating screwing further with the fabric of time and matter.

As soon as the plane landed, he called his therapist and the first thing he asked was for a referral to someone new.

#

Noel got himself a new therapist. Mona had called him asking how his trip to Nebraska was, and he felt the sane and responsible thing to do would be to not call her back.

He told his therapist about how he couldn't get Mona off his mind, and the therapist referred him to a doctor for OCD. The problem wasn't that he was thinking about her, but that every time he tried to put her out of his mind—his psyche would interrupt his thoughts with urges to respond and talk about her.

For two more weeks he journaled and kept his thoughts focused on his own life, and left Mona out of the picture.

The following week he finally felt like moving ahead and went to a Speed Dating night at a local bar. He talked to a few women and finished the night in a positive mood. He didn't stutter. He didn't spit. And anytime he felt like saying, "come again," he literally bit his tongue and just leaned in closer to better hear the things being said.

Things were looking up and he had almost gone a whole month without drinking any more than a single cocktail in a night. Just as he was about to fall asleep one night in his bed and not on the couch after a drunken stupor, he got a phone call. Noel picked up quickly without looking to see who it was because he had just assumed it was his mum and da.

"Noel! I didn't think you would be awake." Mona's voice was coming through the receiver and stirring up anxiety like a hive of angry bees in the pit of his stomach. He reached over for his medication and put a pill beneath his tongue.

"Oh, hey, Mona…" He didn't know how he felt about this. On one hand he knew that inside he still wanted her madly, but on the other, all this woman ever brought him was misery and pain. He thought maybe he could just answer nonchalantly and maybe somehow keep from backsliding.

"Yes, silly. It's me. Didn't you get my message? I was just asking how you were doing."

"I must not have seen it," Noel lied. "I would have called you back..." He tried so hard to pretend like he wasn't still infatuated with her. He didn't just do it for himself he was doing it for her. Wasn't that what she wanted?

"That's fine. I'm sure you were busy. I just wanted to see how you are doing. I went on a few dates with a guy Monique tried to set me up with, and it just made me want to help you find someone. It's nothing serious with me and him, but I—I kinda like him. And, you know, I want that for you, too, Noel."

His blood started to boil. He didn't just get mad; it was as if a switch clicked in his head and he lost all his hard work again. "Really?" That was all he could say. Maybe it was the medication and the weeks of therapy. Maybe it was how hard he was trying, but he couldn't help but think of a million ways to get off the phone. "Listen, Mona. It's good to hear from you, but I really need to get to sleep."

"I understand. I was just calling to see if

you wanted to go do something tomorrow, maybe you can meet William?"

This is the part where he knew he could explode.

"Maybe. Look, why don't you call me in the morning? I really must get to bed. Good night, Mona." He hung up the phone and sat silent for twenty seconds before he realized he wasn't even breathing. He had to say out loud, "Breathe!" to which he added "You OX!"

He had just taken his medication which should have made him tired, but the adrenaline of hearing so much and the mania within his mind made him go to the kitchen and get a bottle of gin. He took one shot and mixed it with more medication. He didn't know what it would do, but he did know it was something he had been warned not to do time and time again.

It didn't matter. He was furious.

He took the paperwork that he had written about how to go about an attempt at restoring reality and burned it in a wastebasket. As he watched the fire settle down, he stamped it out and took a cab to the dreaded machine.

Noel staggered into the storage area and said, "Mona, how'd you like to fail me one more

time!? If I dare you! One more Mona, and you'll
fall for me. One more Mona, and you'll be mine."
He changed the last prototype on the laptop
from a two to a three, showing that he was
going to duplicate her one last time. He walked
over to the switch in a medicated haze and sang
the Rolling Stones song *19th Nervous
Breakdown.*

Between the actual singing and
medication singing its own crazy melody in his
veins, Noel was distracted and closing his eyes
as he pulled the switch.

When they opened, he watched in horror
as a small cat jumped from the top of a nearby
trash can on the keyboard. He'd left the roll up
door wide opened. Stupid, stupid!

But it was too late to do anything about
it. Noel's fingers tingled and the machine
started smoking. There was a loud bang and
Noel fell to the floor unconscious.

Chapter 16

Noel

It was morning to him, but afternoon in the rest of the world. He awoke to the cat licking his face. He was so used to headaches that he just said, "Good morning, bloody headache." He could smell the resonating whiffs of burnt electronics, so he spoke again. "Well and good, Noel! The machine just gave up. You shouldn't have been here in the first place."

As he sat up, he realized parts of his memory were a haze. Why was he here? The last thing he remembered was the phone call from Mona, which wasn't so bad to him in the moment as it was when it had happened. A night of sleep can work wonders. He remembered where he was before she called, and it was such a great place. He remembered feeling angry, but he didn't feel it at all anymore.

Still confused, he pulled the phone from his pocket. He had one message and the battery was all but dead, so he listened to his voicemail. "Hey, good morning, it's Mona. I'm going to the gym. I called it off with William—I was right what I said to you. I'm not intended for a relationship. Let's just go get a coffee—"

He didn't know why he was so happy to hear that. He knew somewhere inside all he wanted to hear was that she loved him back. Noel reasoned that she broke it off with William because she was secretly in love with him, and all he had to do was tell her.

He called her and got her voicemail, "Coffee sounds great—I'm going to catch a cab to the one down by your place and meet you if you are around. I have something I need to tell you!" His phone abruptly died.

Noel had determined he was going to profess his love for her and change everything. He did that thing he had to do when he woke up without a shower and used a cup of water to push down his bed hair. He left the machine behind and locked the storage door. He ran out onto the main street to hail a cab and only saw one person walking on the sidewalk from the distance. It was on the side of town where there were only a few people walking throughout the day, so he expected to see a passerby or two. What he didn't expect to see was Mona. He kept looking closer and closer at the female body coming toward him. She seemed dressed quite oddly with a blue felt hat and stewardess dress, but he was sure as she got closer it had to be her.

"HEY!" He jogged over to her. "I don't know what you are doing on this side of town. It has to be fate."

"I'm listening..." She said back.

"Well, however you got here, whatever reason it is that you showed up, I'm thrilled to have you right where I am! There's something I desperately have to tell you."

"Go ahead."

"I love you. I have always loved you, and I think we are meant to be together. I couldn't bear the thought of seeing you with anyone but me. I like the way you laugh, and the funny things you do. I love the curve of your chin and the way your eyes scrunch up when you laugh."

She peered longingly into his eyes and looked as if she was the happiest woman in the world as he went on.

"I know we have so much in common if we just take the time—" He stopped midsentence as he saw another woman who looked like Mona come jogging down the road with a whistle in her mouth. She blew the whistle and five more women who looked just like Mona came jogging behind her as they all ran past Noel and the woman he was talking to.

"Go on. Go on. You're so sweet. I love you, too. Its love at first sight!" The lady in the stewardess costume was gushing.

Noel just stood there wondering what the hell was happening. Mona was literally everywhere.

The stewardess grabbed him and pulled him into an embrace, but he broke free and ran as fast as he could. He could hear her in the distance shouting, "Don't be afraid. We're meant to be!" She kept following him as her hat fell to the ground and he ran faster to escape.

He turned a corner then and looked up to a billboard and found Mona's face was on it. He hailed a cab to get away from the nightmare and get back home to his medication because he was sure he was seeing things. He told the Iranian cab driver, "Get me out of this neighborhood! Step on it."

The driver answered back, "Sure thing, buddy!" Meanwhile, the stewardess was hot on his trail. She hailed a separate cab and made them follow Noel.

After Noel calmed down, he finally gave the driver directions to his apartment. He was looking out the window at all the people on his street and every woman he saw was just like

Mona. He had the driver stop at the Art Museum and he ran in to see paintings of Mona and the famed Cleopatra sculpture wearing Mona's face.

There were heavy Mona's and skinny Mona's, Black, Asian, and Hispanic Monas, but every woman was her. He knew this had to be a symptom of his OCD. He figured he would just go spend a few days in a hospital and take all the medication he needed. Noel reasoned it would be better to just shut his eyes than to look at the hallucinations he was seeing.

He paid a new cab driver to take him home and he walked like a blind man to his apartment. He felt in the air with his hands and walked through the hallway and up to his apartment. Then, Noel was staggering around his apartment afraid to open his eyes. He went to his medication and took a pill. Immediately, he got into bed and pulled the covers up to his neck. "This is going to be over as soon as you wake up. You just have a bad case of OCD."

He was starting to doze and free himself from the drama when he heard a knock on the door. Who was coming to his apartment on a Sunday? He looked at his alarm clock and saw April 19th then he fumbled through his calendar on the desk and found a small post-it-note that told him his parents would be bringing the puppy by.

"Noel Roll! Are you gonna let me in?" He heard his father's voice through the door, and it was surprisingly reassuring. He opened the door and the small pooch ran into his apartment wagging his tail. "You do remember you're going to watch the puppy for the week while we go out of town don't ya? Your mum is on her way up. You don't do much to keep this place clean these days do you?"

"Dad. I'm not doing the best. Honestly, I don't know if it is a good time to watch the dog."

His Dad kept his jolly demeanor. "Oh! Fiddlesticks. I won't hear of it. Yer going to do what you told us you would do, and you won't have any trouble doin' it. After all, you don't need to go anywhere do ya?"

"Oh my God! Dad. I told this friend I would see her for coffee. I have another hour, but…"

"But nothing. That's fine. Go see your friend. Poochie is going to be alright here. We fed him and let him out on the way up. You have another three hours. He's low maintenance. Just kiss yer mum goodbye for the trip—we're going on our first cruise! Here she comes now."

"Mum? What? You look. Like. Oh my God. I swear I'm losing my mind." His mother wasn't his mother. She was Mona. She was smaller, older, with white hair and soft age lines in the corner of her eyes, but she was Mona none-the-les.

Noel was so frightened he nearly passed out.

"Noel! You've never been so surprised to see me in your life. You look like you've seen a ghost!" His mother's voice sounded different and it was all he could do to keep from running out the door screaming.

"I think I'm losing my mind, Mum." Noel went to his medication and picked up the bottle.

"You don't take those crazy person medications, do you?" His mother was livid. "You need to put down that bottle and give your mother a kiss goodbye. I know you're going through something, but we have to be at the boat in two hours."

"Probably better. Maybe just a hug, Mother. I'll tell you later." Noel kept blinking his eyes deeply in hopes he would wake up from this nightmare.

"Well, I hate leaving you like this." His mother was starting to get protective.

"It's okay. I'll get everything back to normal. Just go have fun. I'm just a little off base today. I'll be better after I get some sleep." He hoped that were true.

"Sounds like it!" His father said as he patted him on the back. "Here's poochie's food and his toys, they're in the bag. You've done this a hundred times. You'll be fine, young man!"

"Uh…Ok. I guess it will be ok. Have fun. I don't know what to say."

Noel ushered his parents out of the apartment, and immediately called Ricardo. "Ricardo! I'm so glad I got ahold of you."

"Noel! Buddy! Things going well?" Ricardo was in great spirits, probably day drinking on a Sunday.

"No, they are not! My mum… She looks like Mona."

Ricardo laughed. "I should say she does. Don't all women kinda look alike?"

"Uh, well, it seems that they do. Yes. They all look like Mona."

"Noel, all women have always looked alike since the dawn of mankind. You're a scientist. You know this. Get a grip, buddy. Why are you suddenly amazed?"

"Don't tell me..."

"Oh, Noel. You think you altered every woman on earth, now don't you? I know this is just a simple progression in your mental health slipping away. I guessed it because I knew you would say something like this next. You keep getting more grandiose about your machine. Destroy that thing! For the love of all that's holy, dismantle it now!"

"But I did this. I really did. I swear."

"Noel, you're making life too complicated. Just take a deep breath. All you must do is accept the world as it is. Just play nice with people. Have a good attitude. You're not God. Is that your parents dog barking? Go down to the coffee shop and take the dog for a walk! You'll feel better after, I promise."

"Oh, shite! I've got to see Mona in an hour. What do I tell her? That I made all the women on earth look just like her?"

"Noel, I don't even know what to say to you anymore... All women look basically the

same! They sound alike, have similar interests…
Why is Mona so special to you? I just can't
understand it. Let her go."

Noel sighed. "You're right. I have done so
many ignorant things to win her over—I might
as well accept this as the only victory I have
going for me."

"That's the Noel I know. Go to therapy
this week. You were starting to do well, and I
don't want to hear about this damned machine
ever again."

"Thanks, buddy," Noel said to Ricardo.

Noel hung up the phone and thought of
how wrong this whole world was. It was a world
of Monas, and he was the only man on the
planet who knew it wasn't the way it was
supposed to be.

It would be pure madness to go about
like things were normal, but what could he do?
If anything, it would take months to build a
machine to fix the whole earth. He sat there
placing formulas in a notebook instead of
getting prepped for coffee with Mona. He
couldn't believe this was the way the chess
pieces had fallen.

He put in a call to Mona, "Hey. Glad you

picked up!"

"I'm glad you called, too. I feel like I have some things to tell you when we meet. You do still want to go to get coffee, right?" Mona seemed like a much more subdued version of herself. He couldn't quite place it, but it seemed as if for the first time she was talking to him with a little twinge of humility.

"I've got a lot to tell you, too!" Noel was realizing that for the first time he might actually have a chance with her. He knew, of course, that now was not the time to come clean with the fact that he made a machine to duplicate her into every woman on earth.

"Great! I'll see you there! Hugs!"

Hugs? This beat the hell out of "buddy." Was this what he was supposed to do to win the damsel? Was he supposed to use his scientific prowess to make the playing field level? He suddenly began to think he wasn't such a fool for doing this in the first place. But, his mother? And, all the women on earth. He sat there with his notebook writing more formulas.

Chapter 17

Noel

The weather was very clear for Chicago. It was eerily dry outside without wind and humidity for once, and it was starting to get just a little warmer. The sun was crystal clear and Noel walked the little vibrant puppy down to the corner café as he waited for Mona. How would he know it was her? Every woman walking on the street was her. He couldn't walk up to every one of them and ask. He decided just to let her find him.

"Noel!" She ran to him and hugged him. "I'm so glad to see you!"

"And you. You look stunning."

"Oh, you've got to be kidding. I look like everyone else."

Noel blinked. It was true. "So modest," he remarked anyway.

She laughed. "You're so funny! That's what I have to tell you. I broke it off with William because I have been wrong to you! I have treated you so badly. I don't have all that ambition, and I don't want to be single my whole life. I want to finish college, but I want you in my life, Noel. I truly do!"

This was too easy. He was winning the woman. He couldn't help but think he had done it in such an egotistical manner. "Don't be so kind, Mona. I do deserve some of it. After all, I am a bit big headed sometimes."

"I don't think so. That just isn't the Noel I know." She winked.

Meanwhile at the other tables in the café were many men talking to Mona-shaped women.

One such clone was writing furiously in a notebook. She sat nearby and Noel thought she might be eavesdropping on their conversation, but he had more pressing matters at hand.

Noel continued, "Well what does this mean? Can we finally go on a real date? They started *Breakfast at Tiffany's* back up at the theater."

"I'd love to, Noel! I want to watch old movies with you. Wait, is that your puppy?" The little dog finally started vying for her attention.

"This is my parent's dog, Poochie. They are going on their first cruise, so I've got to watch him while they're gone." Noel was going on with her, so elated that he could finally tell her about his parents. He didn't even notice that there was a restaurant of waitstaff that looked exactly like her. He was able to tune out the dystopian world that he had created. It was altogether too easy. "I want to tell you, Mona. Things aren't supposed to be like this."

She got a disappointed look on her face. "What do you mean?"

He couldn't stand to burst her bubble. He had wanted to tell her his whole quest to duplicate her right then and there, but he could have died seeing her disappointment. "Oh, I'm supposed to bring you a gift. He went through his pocket and brought out a small box."

"Are you serious? When did you have time to find something?" Mona was thrilled. It was as if the new Mona would love to get Noel's attention just because all women wanted to feel like something special in a world where looks didn't matter.

"I stopped on the way. It was such a pretty day, and it's just a little gift. It will look great on you."

She opened the box and saw a small necklace with charms.

"Oh, that's so kind, Noel. I will treasure it, just like you treat me like a treasure. I don't understand what you see in me.”

It was starting to tick Noel off that Mona was so humble. It had always been one of the things that attracted him to her, that she was full of spite and so independent. Yet, he shrugged it off because he was happy to be with her. “I’m working on a huge project. I don’t want to tell you everything about it, but I’m going to make some pretty big changes with my new scientific breakthrough.” Noel was feeling better about himself as he tried to rectify the issues he had so harshly screwed with.

“I’m so glad to hear that. Can I count on seeing you some time before our date to see the movie?”

“If you wanted to be around me at all, you should know I’m always here for you. I met you and did everything I could to be with you, Mona. So, just getting time with you is all I want.”

“That’s so sweet. You must be the kindest man in the world. Oh, damn. I have to go to class. Do you want to meet Monique later this evening?”

Noel wasn’t so thrilled about meeting another woman who looked like her. It was just weird, but he had always wanted to meet her friend. In some quirky way it was part of their new love life. "I'd love to meet her. Bring her to my place tonight! I'm going to be working on my project every day until I can get things right."

"What do you mean get things right?" Mona finally had started listening to every word he said. Normally, she would have just let his words fly past her.

"Oh. I'll explain later. It's too much to tell you now, and I am just so happy to hear you want to finally date!"

"I'm glad you're happy. See you soon. Hugs." She kissed him on the cheek. And Noel turned red. This had to be the best day of his life. But it was in so many ways the worst day as well. He had so much to fix. He would be working in his laboratory for months to save his butt from being the worst mad scientist in the world.

He took Poochie home and began to relax on the couch writing more and more formulas. He would write a whole page and use the pencil eraser to the point of tearing a hole in the notebook paper. He was driving himself mad on one of the best days of his adult life. It had to feel completely bittersweet and he hated it as much as he loved it. He just didn't want to take the time to figure out whether he loved it or hated it because he was becoming numb to his own neurosis.

#

That night he got a buzzing on his door around seven and he put down his hours of obsessive work. "Mona!" She walked through the door and kissed him fully on the lips. He wondered for a second why it was so personal all of the sudden, but it could be anything. He was with the woman of his dreams.

She was wearing the necklace from earlier, but her dress was one he hadn't seen her in before. He couldn't help but think her style was something quite different from her usual attire. It was a bold red dress with sequins and it just screamed flamboyant. She had never been this loud with her styling choices before. "That dress is something else." Noel didn't know what to say. "Where's Monique?"

"Monique?" She seemed completely puzzled.

He wondered if her memory had gotten lost in the transition of the world last night. "Yes, don't you remember, Mona? You said you were bringing Monique."

"Oh, yeah. I do remember. No, she had to be somewhere else." Her normal accent was gone. It was as if she had a lazy demeanor. Noel was beginning to wonder if she was drunk.

"Well. It's no problem. I did want to meet her, but we can watch a movie—I have *An Affair to Remember*. How about that one?"

"What's that about?" She was chewing on gum and he had never noticed her to talk so nonchalantly before.

"You haven't heard of it?" Noel was beginning to wonder if she was anything at all like she had been before. "It's a classic."

"Oh. I don't want to watch an old movie. Maybe we could watch a horror flick, something scary?" This didn't seem like Mona at all. He was beginning to question what the game was.

She sat next on the couch very un-lady like. She was woman-spreading with her miniskirt and he oddly was not attracted to the whole scene. It was as if there was a little bit of a challenge to Mona in the past. They turned on the movie and she wouldn't get off of him. She kept making out with him nonstop. It was as if she was in heat. Noel kept asking if she wanted something to drink or something to eat, and she wouldn't get off him. He wondered what was

going on until he finally heard a ring at his door
again. "Let me get that."

"No. Don't worry about it. They will go
away." She was nervous. He was beginning to
think about throwing her out and scrapping his
dreams of Mona when he insisted and went for
the door.

Standing at the door was a darker
skinned Mona clone in a jogging suit with duct
tape around her wrists. "It's me, Monique! That
is not Mona. Mona and I are being held at the
base of the stairs!" She was talking so
frantically.

"Who are you?" Noel was beginning to get
stern with the lady on the couch. "Where's
Mona?"

"Noel! It's me. You told me you loved me."
The woman was pleading for him with
everything but tears.

"I don't know you! Who are you?
Monique. I don't know this woman."

Monique spoke up again. "Don't worry
she's crazy. She told us everything. She has
been stalking you all day. Just come get us out
of here and call the police!"

"Alright! That's just what I'm going to

do." He reached for his phone and the stewardess stalker started to run out the door. "Wait! The necklace! Give it back or, or, I'll hit you with this lamp." He had no plans of striking her, but he knew she was a few cards short of a deck. She took off the necklace and ran down the stairs and they watched out the window as she took a cab.

Noel went down to meet Mona, "Oh, my God! Mona?" He removed her duct tape and untied Monique, too. "Are you okay?"

"Yes. That was horrific." Mona was breathing heavily. "She was there at the café, she must have heard everything we said. I recognized her."

"How did you?" Noel was being a bit sarcastic because he wondered truthfully how anyone could recognize anyone. "Never mind. This is all my fault."

Monique spoke up. "Oh, don't blame yourself. She was a freak!"

"No. I made women all look the same. I did it. It was me."

"What are you talking about?" Mona chimed.

"Yes. I was trying not to tell you, but I

made a machine. And. And. I got drunk. And I made all the women on earth look like you."

"That's crazy Noel. You can't do something like that. Women have always looked the same." Mona was trying to calm him down.

"No, why does everyone keep saying that? Women haven't always looked the same. And. My mother. This is going too far…"

Mona looked disappointed. "Noel. You have too many issues. I can't see you if you think these crazy delusions."

"Mona. No! You have to believe me. I will show you the machine."

Mona grabbed Monique by the hand, looking at Noel. "I'm afraid we can't see each other anymore. Don't call me." She was about to leave, and he stopped her.

"Please, Mona." Noel had the saddest eyes in the world. "Take this necklace. You mean the world to me. I can quit talking like this if it makes you feel better. You're never going to believe me, anyway."

Monique took the necklace and handed it to Mona.

Mona firmly told him, "I don't know. I

can't right now." Mona and Monique left him, and he just slouched drearily, the most defeated he had ever been.

Chapter 18

Noel

The world was mad. It was completely upside down and it was his fault. The only silver lining he could find was that one Mona among the thousands had actually liked him, well, two actually had, but one was insane and possibly homicidal.

There was no one he knew who could understand what he had done and help him pick up the pieces. Then he remembered... That wasn't true. There was somebody.

"Teresa? Dr. Teresa Helms? It's me, Noel Kensington, your old college buddy. You'll never believe this, but I have some formulas that you have got to see. It's going to blow the world of physics out of the water. Just please make the time to see me. I'll fly to you. Call me back."

Two days went by when the phone finally rang, waking Noel from his purgatory. "Noel! How are you, friend?" Her voice was slightly different than it was in college. He dreaded what he had done to her. She wasn't his type, but she was aesthetically pleasing in her own right, and it almost defeated him to hear the fruits of his botched experiment.

Teresa wasn't Teresa anymore. Thanks to Noel, she was Mona, too.

Noel was talking so quickly she had to interrupt him a few times. He explained everything and her could hear her writing down his formulas in a notepad. "That's intriguing, Noel. What you're saying is it is possible to change the fabric of genetic makeup, and you had a failed attempt that brought about all of this? Send me the paperwork, and pictures of your machine." She was the only person who had believed him so far, and it was completely comforting.

"Yes. I'm sending them now. They're on my phone." He uploaded the documents to her by email and she brought them up on her computer screen at home.

"This is mad science, Noel. I wouldn't have pictured you doing anything like this. This could change everything for the field of physics. How can you just sit on this?" She was ready to make the discovery public right then and there.

"No. I don't want to be connected to this." Noel didn't want the world to think him a monster.

"I'm sending this to the publisher, but I'll keep your name out of it. Why do you want me to make this public anyway, you're obviously a little embarrassed?"

"The same reason I made the machine in the first place. She doesn't believe me."

Teresa sucked her teeth. "You are truly mad. Everything you do is for her. So, tell me, what did I look like before?"

"You—well, you had a long, graceful neck, and there was a tiny mole near your left ear. It—it is a total travesty, what I have done. I will get you back to normal, Teresa. Just do what you can so that she believes me."

"I've got Popular Science in a chat window as we speak and they want to do an exclusive," Teresa said.

"This is big, and dumb. This is the dumbest thing I have ever done."

He went to his storage space and tinkered with his machine for weeks on end. It had been two weeks since Mona had been taken hostage by her clone, and he finally felt it important to contact her. It had blown up on the news that there was something "fundamentally wrong" with the "cosmos" in that every woman had the same appearance. Mona had to have heard the news since it was the biggest thing mentioned in the media in years. Most outlets ran "an unknown experiment has altered the appearance of every woman ever born."

He got her voice mail. "Mona, it's me, stupid Noel. I did it. I made my findings public so you could see that I'm not lying. Will you give me another chance? I don't see why you would, but I'm going to make things right. Now you know what that means. I know I'm barely making sense. Please forgive me."

He went back to working on his machine and writing in his notebook for two hours when finally, Mona called him back. He picked up on the first ring.

"Noel. This is crazy." She started slowly, "I have to be just as crazy as you to be calling you back. Why would you do such a crazy thing? They are saying that all women look and sound and even smell exactly the same because of an experiment gone horribly wrong, and I know it had to be you who did it. Can you tell me more about this?"

"I did it, Mona. It was an accident. I tried to clone you so I could have a chance with you. The original Mona refused all relationships, so I thought if I made another one, a carbon copy, if you will, that one Mona would have me. I just loved you so much. I would have done anything for a chance."

"What woman is going to say yes to a man that insane?"

"I know. I wouldn't blame you if you never spoke to me again, but if you come spend time with me—I'll fix this. We just need to do one last thing and my machine will restore things."

"You are some kind of mad scientist, Noel Kensington!"

"I know, but you're talking to me, still, and I have no idea why."

"That makes two of us! I went on that date with William and all I could think about was you. Your accent—the way we met. I loved everything about you, and you just did everything wrong!"

"I know. But I'm going to make it right."

"The thing I can't get over, is that I have missed you terribly over the last two weeks. I think I would love you in any world. Whether it's one where I'm the only Mona, and one where there are ten of me and twenty of you."

Noel couldn't believe his ears. "Wow! I

don't believe it."

"I have always loved you. I just tried to pretend I could be cool about it. I was trying to turn you away because it was the only way I could hide what I feel."

"I love you, too."

"Just come get me, and we'll fix this machine of yours. We'll do it together."

She hung up and all Noel could do was cry tears of joy. He was certain in his heart of hearts that Mona had felt this way even when there was only one of her in the entire universe. She just refused to admit it to herself. If she could forgive him now after all he had done, those feelings had to be strong.

He put all his work on hold and sped to get to her. By the time he had arrived he wondered if it was all too good to be true and whether it was all a pretty delusion.

Mona was standing in her doorway, looking perfect with her heart-shaped face and auburn hair. Noel rushed to get to her and said, "How do I know it's you? What's something only you know? There is a stalker out there, less we forget."

Mona smiled. "Noel, we met at Versace,

and I saw you in your first therapy session. That woman was arrested. Hopefully she's getting the help she needs." She stroked his shoulder "You really can't tell the difference between women, can you?"

Noel sighed hopefully. "I'm just not as used to it as you are. Come here, Mona!" He hugged her and shared a deep kiss. His last kiss had been with an imposter. There they held each other in the hallway: two lovebirds with a most unique story.

Noel knew it was her. She was the Mona he had always dreamed of holding. She seemed just as happy to be held.

"Noel," she said, touching his face "I want to tell you now all the things I was too afraid to say before. You're so clever, so talented. You're not afraid to feel things and you can be so selfless sometimes. I never told you that. You always put me first, even when I was a jerk. No wonder you went so overboard. We were meant to be together, I feel it in my bones, and you just did everything you could to get to me, while I tried to stay out of reach. Some men say they will swim an ocean. You would fill the world up with *me* to have my love. We're going to fix this machine and get things back the way they are supposed to be, together."

Noel caressed her chin. "Um. That's just it. We need chemicals and a part for the machine that you can only find in the local college lab, and I have no way of getting them. I have been at an impasse for days, but we're going to have to break-in to the lab."

Mona bit her lip. "Oh, that's exciting. Let's go on our first adventure!"

He couldn't believe she was so ready to be involved in his wild world with him. His whole life was coming together at long last.

"So, you don't like your mother looking like me?" Mona joked.

"You've got to be kidding."

"I am."

"There's only one you, and I'm not sure if you're going to remember a thing after we fix the machine… From what I have written on the topic, I'm almost a hundred percent sure you'll forget all about this reality and one more only I will know about it."

Mona swallowed hard; her voice thick with tears. "Are you afraid I'm not going to be in love with you? Noel, I promise, I have always cared about you. You believe me, don't you?"

Noel touched her hair. "I want to believe that, but this is all so strange. How can I count on anything? Let's get some ski masks and break into the local college because that's what two people who just fell in love always do." He winked.

"Yeah. I'm with you on that. We should wait until midnight."

"Together!"

They talked for hours and grabbed a few old movies from the rental box. It was eye opening to see movies in which she was the lead actress. In this world, every woman was Mona, from Marilyn Monroe to Scarlet Johansson. He watched old classics where every female lead was a Mona look alike. They threw popcorn at each other and laughed nonstop. No one would have ever known that they were so right together, but Mona could be so sweet when she let her guard down. They kissed a few times and it was like magic. There was so much chemistry and they both wanted to go further together, but they had decided, each one, to wait until the earth had been repaired to stir up their physical attractions.

At midnight it was time to move and do the thrilling break-in at the chemistry lab.

It was a standard smash and grab, and they walked like cat burglars up to the door and Mona surprised him by picking the lock. "How the hell do you know how to pick a lock?" Noel was so amazed he had to inquire.

She whispered, "You'll never believe this. My parents used to move so much from house to house that they didn't remember to give me a key and one time I was locked out of my own house until I learned to pick the lock. I've been able to do it ever since."

He whispered back, "I can't learn enough about you. You are so funny, Mona. Just yesterday I thought you hated me."

"I know. I should never have lied to myself like that, but..." they lifted their masks to kiss and went into the lab. Noel read all the labels and poured chemicals from one flask into another while she watched down the hallway.

"Someone's coming," she whispered.

"I'm almost done." Just then the lights were switched on, and a female security guard sauntered into the lab.

"I got you two! What are you trying to steal?" She was a little beefier than Mona but she was a Mona clone nonetheless.

The two lovers just laughed together because they were thrilled to get caught. It was not a huge crime, and they thought they could probably talk their way out of it. They were so in love that they thought the world loved them back. The security guard kept talking, "Hold it right there! I'm going to have to take you two in—"

At just that moment Mona and the security guard started singing *We've Only Just Begun* from the middle of the song. Noel's eyes went wide. It was happening again.

Mona and the guard were halfway through their chorus when Noel grabbed Mona by the arm and pulled her away from her strange concert. The security guard was still singing, and Noel didn't question it as they both made their getaway, cracking up together with a bag full of the chemicals and the missing part for the machine.

Only Mona could inspire a world where all she wanted to do was sing with herself.

Chapter 19

Noel

Mona spent the next week avoiding her classes. She had the top grades anyway, so she had earned a break to spend with her new man. She had a chair in his storage space and would read her homework aloud to Noel while he tinkered away at the machine.

"How do you know so much about Psychology, Noel Roll?" She insisted on being cute and calling him Noel Roll when she found out his father did that. He normally would have cringed, but he was happy for her to say his name any way she wanted.

Noel kidded, "I learned about it over the last few months. I am what you would call self-taught." They laughed. They had already discussed that the world outside would think they were the worst couple with their manic adventures and their delusionary love story. Yet, they'd gotten so close over the last week. They knew they wouldn't be spending all their time together in the future, but it was much like a love vacation.

"I'm almost through with this machine. We're going to pull the switch at the same time. That is the only way we can both remember

everything that happened. And, on top of that—
I'm not sure it will work for both of us, Mona."
He gazed at her adoringly, wiping some grime
onto his pants. "So, if this is the last moment I
get with you, and you never want to be with me
again... Screw it, just kiss me!" They held each
other so close.

"Oh, Noel," Mona said. "I know the way I
feel is so real that it will last over a million
lifetimes, no matter what the outcome of this
next experiment is."

They counted to three and both switched
the switch, and nothing happened. Noel reset
the switch and spoke one more time, "Okay. I
forgot to press one button on the computer.
Sorry." They kissed again and they both pulled
the switch again. A surge of energy went
through their bodies and they both fell to the
ground in each other's arms.

It was hours later that Noel woke up to
find Mona lying in his arms. He checked and
she was breathing as she just barely spoke and
rolled over to sleep some more. Placing a jacket
over her while she slept, he took a quick walk
around the corner and found that women were
back to normal. They were all different once
more.

He went running back to her and

screamed loudly. "Mona! It worked! It worked!"

She woke up and said, "Noel? What am I doing here? What is this place?"

Noel gripped the hair of his head tightly between his fingers. "You don't remember anything?" He was distraught. All the worlds he had been through to get her meant nothing if she didn't fall for him.

Mona yawned. "I remember you saying you wanted to show me your machine and all it did was zap me. Noel, I could have been hurt."

He stopped pulling his hair and scratched his ear. "So we never kissed?"

"Never kissed? Don't be silly. We've been dating for weeks!" She smiled at him and held his hand.

"I'm puzzled." He didn't know what to think. What had changed? What hadn't?

Her smile spread slowly across her heart-shaped face. "I'm just kidding with you. I remember it all."

Noel scooped Mona up in his arms and squeezed her tightly

She laughed, "Did you fix the world? I

know that's a weird question to ask."

"Yes, I fixed it. I mean I have to check everything, but it seems back to normal. Which world do you remember? Do you remember living in a world where you were every woman and every woman was you?"

"What are you talking about?" She frowned.

"You don't know—" He pulled back and looked her in the eye.

She swatted at him playfully. "I'm just kidding, I remember both worlds, and like I told you, Noel Kensington, I will love you in any world. We're meant to be."

Noel gave Mona a hearty squeeze. "I love you, but please stop doing that. My heart can't take it."

Mona kissed Noel on the nose. "Sorry, it was just too easy."

They held each other for hours and only stopped long enough for Noel to smash the machine to bits.

Chapter 20

Mona

Over the course of the following days, Mona began moving some of her things into Noel's apartment. Not only was she just about finished with her classes for the semester, but she'd even taught Poochie how to roll over.

Some nights the three of them would play on the floor in front of the TV, giving a whole new meaning to the term Noel Roll, with Mona, the puppy, and the man of her dreams spinning across the floor with belly laughs and kisses.

Noel was on the couch putting the finishing touches on his latest thesis and Mona was at the dining table scratching down some notes for one of her own. She gazed at him adoringly, recalling how he'd turned the world upside down just for a chance to be with her.

When she couldn't stand it anymore, Mona rushed over to his side and messed his hair, kissing him again on the nose.

"Noel, can I ask you something?"

"Sure, babe, what is it?"

"Well, it's just that there was a time not so very long ago that all you wanted in the world was more Mona," she laughed and rubbed his back.

He smiled. "You're right about that."

"So, my question is, you've got more Mona now than you ever bargained for... Do you...do you have any regrets?"

Noel looked into her eyes for a very long time, then he said, "never. I almost had a nervous breakdown to get here." He gave her a squeeze. "But I wouldn't change a thing."

THE END

Acknowledgments:

Thank you for reading my fourth book, More Mona. If you enjoyed it, please leave a review on Amazon. You must acquire reviews to promote your book and hopefully sell it. It would mean so much if you helped.

Thanks to Sasha McBrayer for healing the book with her amazing editing skills, and special thanks to Amy Tate Photography for providing the Author Picture.

Also, thanks to my readers everywhere. With your support I can continue to do what I love.

Rob J. Blevins